THE CLOCK WORK ALICE

DEANNA KNIPPLING

WONDERLAND PRESS
LITTLETON, CO

The Clockwork Alice

Published by Wonderland Press
Littleton, Colorado, USA

First printing, June 2017

Discover more by this author at www.Wonderlandpress.com.

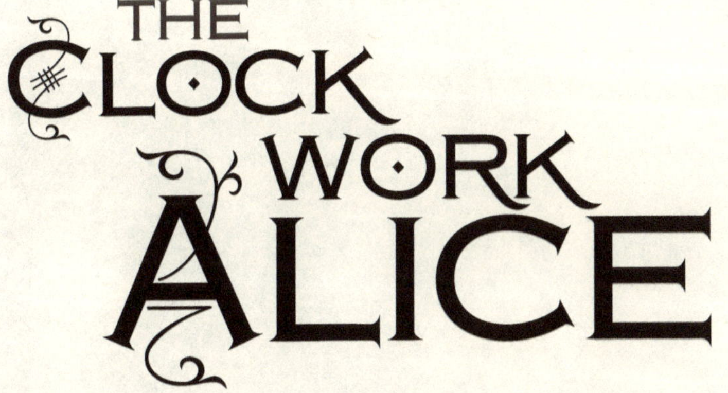
THE
CLOCK
WORK
ALICE

A Brief History

of Alice

Where did the book *Alice's Adventures in Wonderland* begin?

It may have begun with a senior member of Christ Church College at Oxford University named Charles Lutwidge Dodgson, who turned his name into a cipher and became Lewis Carroll.

It may have begun with a little girl named Alice Liddell, the daughter of Henry Liddell, the Dean of Christ Church college—and Charles Dodgson's boss.

It may have begun when Charles Dodgson met Alice in 1856, when Alice was four years old and the Reverend Dodgson twenty-four, so that he could take a photograph—he was one of the earliest photographers, and a good one—of her and her sisters Edith (aged two) and Ina (aged seven). Mrs. Liddell, who had married above herself, was known to be a social climber with a short temper.

It may have begun in 1862, when Reverend Dodgson told Alice, Ina, and Edith (along with their chaperone, the Reverend Robinson Duckworth) the earliest form of the story on a boat trip of the Isis.

It may have begun when, at Alice's insistence, Reverend Dodgson presented the girls with a hand-lettered and -illustrated version of the story, *Alice's Adventures Under Ground*, in November of 1864.

At any rate, it began.

Shortly after the writing of *Alice's Adventures Under Ground*, the Reverend Dodgson was banished from the family circle for mysterious reasons, which Mrs. Liddell may have worked to further obscure.

Later, when Alice was seventeen, despite the fact that the break had not been repaired, Reverend Dodgson was asked to take portraits of Ina and Alice once more. Ina's photograph is that of a self-assured know-it-all with a direct if somewhat spoilt gaze and an intellectual finger laid beside her chin. Alice's expression is different. Under her intricate hairdo, she is a petulant, dissatisfied young woman whose head appears to be in danger of falling off her neck, she is so dreadfully *bored* with the proceedings.

Happy she was not.

In 1871, two years after the final photograph, Dodgson published *Through the Looking-Glass*. The White Knight, often thought to be a representation of Dodgson himself, escorts Alice through a small part of the chessboard; then they part, never to meet again.

Alice was rumored to be in love with the youngest son of Queen Elizabeth, a boy named Leopold. Leopold was under pressure from the queen to marry a princess—the fact that this princess was a cousin didn't matter.

Edith passed in 1876; Leopold was one of her pall-bearers. The same year, Dodgson published the mysterious long poem (and possible logic puzzle) *The Hunting of the Snark*.

Four years later, Alice wed a wealthy cricketer and son of a mill-owner named Reginald Hargreaves. Alice and Reginald lived in a large, nearly palatial estate in Hampshire named Cuffnells; it was demolished in the early 1950s after being used as a hotel and a home for a searchlight battalion during World War II, and is known as one of the lost country-houses of England. One of the fireplaces is said to survive at a nearby inn.

Reverend Dodgson did not attend Alice's wedding, although he sent her a watercolor of Tom Quad, the heart of Christ Church college at Oxford, once their shared home. The same year, he gave up photography (although that probably had more to do with the cost of keeping up with new technology than anything else).

Alice had three sons: Alan Knyveton (1881), Leopold Reginald (1883), and Carryl Liddell (1887). Alan and Rex were killed in World War I.

Leopold finally married his princess, Helene Friederike of Waldeck and Pyrmont, in 1882. Leopold fathered a daughter, Alice—supposedly named after his older sister—in 1883. Leopold died in 1884 of a tumble down stairs that might have occurred due to joint pain from his hereditary hemophilia. A second son, Charles Edward, was born to his wife after his death.

In 1895, Dodgson published the popularly disappointing *Sylvie and Bruno*. He died three years later at his sister's home, with Henry Liddell, Alice's father, passing only a few days later.

Alice died in 1934, age eighty-two. She had been born in the first half of the Victorian era, yet lived to see the birth of electric lights, automobiles, and quantum mechanics.

After her death, she was cremated—almost as though, even if the trumpets sounded and the Savior returned—she did not wish to come back.

Notes

on a Mad Universe:

1. To travel through a Direction is also to travel through Time; likewise, in order to travel through Time, one must follow a complex maze of Direction;

2. Sunset on one side of the world is still sunset on the other side of the world, even though there is only one sun and two sides of (the essentially flat) Wonderland;

3. Only Time can repair a broken heart, but not all Time, only a particular kind of Time that must be reached via routes which may or may not have been Lost;

4 Water is a Direction and not merely a State of Matter. Other items may possess an element of Water: mirrors, paintings, doorways, archways, rabbit-holes, dreams;

5 The Red Queen and the Queen of Hearts may or may not have been the same person, historically speaking, but there is only one of them now, and she possesses the memories of both. There is probably a story behind that state of events, but I do not know it, and the Red Queen is unlikely to admit of it as a Question, let alone provide an Answer with any modicum of truth;

6 "North is six, South is three, West is twelve, and all the rest should be obvious," as the Red Queen once said;

7 Although she may have been lying.

"For the snark *was* a boojum, you see."
— Lewis Carroll, "The Hunting of the Snark"

Part I — NINE O'CLOCK —

EAST — SUMMER — UPSIDE-DOWN —

NEXT SUNDAY

In Wonderland, one only works in one's sleep.

All proper Wonderlandians spend all night, every night, hard at work winding the great clock of Wonderland, the Master Chronometer, of which all other Wonderlandians are but synchronized slave clocks.

At night, one understands that one is made of clockwork, although of course one pretends otherwise when one is awake. To do otherwise would make the current madness of the daylit Wonderlandians look like stark sanity.

Besides, it's only polite.

—

The White Rabbit's main duty was to carry reports between the two main courts of Wonderland, the Red Queen's Court and the Golden Court. (The White Court had long since wandered into philosophical territories along the meandering coastline, no one knew quite where.) In order to accomplish this purpose, he had been given a new pocket-watch to replace his old one, and that served as a safe-conduct and prevented him from having to obey certain laws that affected the other Wonderlandians. Alas, no-one paid the slightest amount of attention to him, which meant that he was both the perfect messenger for traveling through dangerous territory, yet completely useless once he had arrived.

Being an earnest Rabbit, he attempted to warn both courts of the dangerous gossip he heard while traveling—that the populace of both the daylit and moonlit Wonderlands were very near to uprising, following a mysterious leader who spread rumors of something known as *The Great Unwinding.*

They ignored him.

He ran faster and tried harder to gain the attention of the two courts, and for a time it seemed almost as though they were listening to him—which may have been a mistake.

But then two clerks of the Golden Court caught up to him as he was carrying messages to and fro (you can tell that he was severely overworked because he was required to do both), and arrested for lack of sleep. This was a serious offense in Wonderland, and exactly the thing that the White Rabbit, as a lifelong bureaucrat, had come to expect: the tyranny of paradox.

The White Rabbit, in order to attract the attention of both courts, must work both day *and* night; and yet if he did not spend the proper amount of time each night winding the Master Chronometer, all the clockwork in Wonderland would slowly lose time (at least in theory), and no one could tolerate *that*.

And so, the harder the White Rabbit worked to save Wonderland, the more in debt of sleep he became.

The punishment for sleeplessness was death.

Pending trial, the White Rabbit was imprisoned at the top the needle-like tower that lay in the center of the Central Palace, which rested upon the Mainspring of the Great Chronometer.

No-one particularly liked the White Rabbit; no one particularly noticed that he was no longer gadding about except the Red Queen, who had one fewer Wonderlandian to shout at on a regular basis. When the other members of the courts heard what had happened, they scoffed.

"What good are reports?" said the Wonderlandians. "Just gossip. The Master Chronometer never falters; it's just the White Rabbit trying to make himself look important again."

—

Alice was sitting above the riverbank with her sister, Ina; she was supposed to be reading Sermons, which unfortunately upset her stomach, so she was eating cherries and drawing figures in the dirt instead, with a forked stick.

"Alice!" cried her sister. "Your hands are covered in blood!"

Alice looked down at her hands, but it was only cherry juice they were covered in. She protested as much to her sister.

Her sister did not find this the least bit comforting. "Wash your hands off this instant or you'll stain your book!"

Alice did not see how she would be able to wash her hands *off*, at least not without making the mess worse than it already was, but she scooted down to the riverbank and dipped her hands into the water anyway, her sister being less than rational where books were involved.

Unfortunately the cherry juice had stained her hands, and there was no removing it.

She began to scrub her hands with sand from the riverbank, hoping at least to lighten the stains enough that they could be concealed by a pair of gloves—the juice had gone almost up to her elbows—but when she had finished her scrubbing, her hands were red still.

"I shall have to tell Ina that they are red for ever," Alice said to herself. "I wonder if she will tell Mother that I'm a murderer, for it's only murderers who have hands stained the color of blood in stories."

Alice leaned back on her heels and started to stand in order to climb up the riverbank, but was interrupted by a splash in the river.

Swimming weakly in the water in front of her was a rabbit. Not, as she had suddenly hoped, the White Rabbit who had once led her to Wonderland, but a brown one, with a brown coat, blue tie, and eyes bulging with fright.

He was a poor swimmer; in fact, it seemed as if he were about to drown.

"The March Hare!" Alice cried, then clapped both hands over her mouth, lest Ina take note. However, Ina only glanced up for a moment, then turned a page and went back to her book.

As soon as it was safe, Alice reached down and pulled the March Hare out of the river, and dragged him onto the bank.

He lay gasping on the sand, face down, his arms and legs spread wide as if he were clinging to the ground itself. "I'm late…I'm late…" he said.

Alice rolled him onto his back, then helped him to sit up. "Marchy! Whatever brings you out of Wonderland?"

"It was…terrible…mistake," he gasped. "Thought… White Rabbit…mocked…abused…so wrong…"

She gave him a cherry, which he ate greedily, smearing red juice all over his mouth and paws. He reached out for another, still gasping for air. Soon, however, he was able to speak.

"The White Rabbit has been arrested," he whispered, peering over Alice's shoulder at her sister, who was still reading her book.

"By the Red Queen? Is he all right? Has his head been cut off already? If so, I don't think I can do anything for him," said Alice.

"Not the Red Queen at all, but by the clerks of the Golden Court," the March Hare explained. "He worked so hard to try to convince the Red Queen and the Crown—that's the Crown that Watches over the Golden Court—that there *was* something to all the rumors of the Great Unwinding— and we did not believe him—and now he has been con- demned to death for letting his accounts with the Master Chronometer fall into such arrears."

Alice hadn't the slightest idea what he was talking about, but the situation was soon explained, at least in part. When she had heard that the Wonderlandians were in actuality made of clockwork, she touched the March Hare on the ear, which felt exactly as warm and soft as that of any nor- mal rabbit.

He flicked his ear and gave her a cross look. "Stop that!"

"Sorry." A question occurred to her. "But why is it so im- portant that the White Rabbit be rescued from the Golden Court? He is only the old White Rabbit after all."

"That's what we all thought," said the March Hare. "And the truth is that the explanation was so confusing that I haven't the slightest idea at all what it means. But in short the Red Queen called for you to come, Alice, and it was either fetch your head to attend her or leave mine behind entirely."

Alice nodded; she could quite understand his point of view on the matter. "I shall come with you and find out what it is that has happened, if I must," she said, not mentioning the red stain on her hands, the sermon, or her sister. "But do you know how to get back to Wonderland from here? "

"Of course," the March Hare said, looking insulted. "You have only to—"

She put a finger against his cherry-stained mouth. "Shush," she said. "I don't wish to be any more confused than I am already. Don't explain, just lead on. When people begin to explain things, it only makes my head ache."

The Golden Court is a dreadful place!" cried the Red Queen. "Filled with beetles, brass men, and barbarians! And of course all of us must slave there every night, from highest to lowest, which hardly seems fair!"

The March Hare had soon led Alice to the Red Queen's Court, which looked nothing like it had the previous times that Alice had been there; now it appeared to be placed on the bough of an enormous cherry tree, with lights twinkling along the branches. The leaves rustled continuously, both from the breeze and from the squirrels wearing red waistcoats, running along the branches.

Alice was soon brought to the Red Queen's throne, which was an enormous, intricately carved chair that had been cut into the trunk of the tree in a kind of archway where the bark had been peeled back. Drips of cherry-sap flowed along the edges of the archway; the Red Knave, standing at ease near the archway, would dip his finger into them whenever he thought the Queen wasn't looking, and take a long, insouciant lick.

The Red King, who looked more than half-asleep in his smaller throne next to the Queen's, muttered, "Not *all* of us, you know."

"Silence!"

The day was getting on. It was already the latest that Alice had been in Wonderland, and the sun was setting with a red glow amongst the clouds, which were in the shapes of puffed hearts. The lights under the branches proved to be glow-bugs, which bobbed and wove around everyone's heads, sometimes crawling about in the wigs of the taller members of the court.

"It is almost time for us to begin our slavery," said the Red Queen. "So you must be given the pocket-watch right away."

She took a deep breath, and Alice covered her ears. Even so, she could easily hear the Red Queen shriek.

"Hatta!"

From the distance along one of the branches overhead came a rustle of leaves, then a pounding sound and a trail of smoke. Alice followed it along the branch, then gasped as a tiny figure leapt off the high branch and plummeted down toward their own.

With a crash the figure landed and straightened its hat: for it was none other than the Mad Hatter, bearing an enormous, dripping pocket-watch.

January 4, 1900; Cuffnells Estate, Hampshire, England

Alice Hargreaves sat straight up in bed—a sound had startled her out of a deep and dreamless sleep. She was convinced that she had just heard the sound of a clock ticking—a monstrous clock, one that had shaken her awake.

But it was not; it was only Reginald's pocket-watch, and it was not even within her room, but in Reginald's dressing-chamber, two rooms away.

She looked around the bedroom but saw nothing amiss; the door to Reginald's room was slightly ajar, that was all. Reginald was sound asleep in the bed beside her; he had been having nightmares lately, and she would often wake to find that he had slipped from his room into hers, as silently as if he had simply appeared there. *He* had not woken her; his breath puffed out of his lips with the undignified hush of deep sleep.

She slid back down into the covers, drawing them back up over her shoulder, and tried to go back to sleep, pressing her back against Reginald's in the bed.

However, the room was over-bright with moonlight; she had forgotten to close the curtains when she had gone to bed, and now the face of the moon watched her, as if curious to see into her dreams.

"Shush," she told it. "Watch if you like, but only be quiet."

She forced her eyes closed.

Once Alice had caught her breath from the Mad Hatter's extraordinary leap, she rushed forward to embrace him. "Hatter!" she cried. "How glad I am to see you."

"You are?" He squinted at her through his monocle.

It was such a relief to see a familiar face that she *was* glad. It had been a long time since she had been in Wonderland, and any familiar face was to be cherished. "Of course," she said.

"Never mind that," the Red Queen said. "We haven't the time for niceties!"

Hatter held up the watch and shook it, as if to suggest that rather there was.

The Red Queen snatched the watch away from him and thrust it toward Alice, who was forced to catch it in both arms, it was so big.

"North is six, South is three, West is twelve, and all the rest should be obvious," the Queen said. "And you must never forget—"

Just then the glow-bugs flashed brightly and burnt themselves into little puffs of smoke, and went out.

When Alice had blinked her eyes clear of the smoke (which stung her eyes to tears), she saw that everyone else had vanished, too—the Red Queen, the Red King, the Red Knave, the March Hare (who had been leaning against the trunk and picking his teeth with a twig), the Mad Hatter, and everyone else who had been standing about, including the squirrels.

"What shall I do?" asked Alice. "I am to save the White Rabbit from the Golden Court, that is clear, but where that is or how I shall get there—or even *why* the White Rabbit must be saved—is such a mystery that I can't think of where to begin."

Always, when Alice had previously been in Wonderland, events had come upon her so fast and thick that she had been quite unable to make sense of them, but she had always known what to do, not least because things were being done to her that she didn't like, and she would not put up with *that*. Or else it was perfectly obvious where she wanted to go—to the Garden, or to the Eighth Square, for example—and she had only to follow whatever direction it was that was pointed out to her. Or *else* she would blink or doze off, and she would wake somewhere else, perhaps on a railway-car, perhaps in a green forest. Everyone in Wonderland was always popping about.

Only once had she been truly stuck, and that had been when she had first come to Wonderland, with the golden key on the table, and the door to the garden too small to fit through. *Then* she had wept, and been carried out of the room in a direction she hadn't expected, but at least she had known which way she wished to go—not that she had been able to go that way, but at least she had *known.*

Now, she could go anywhere along the boughs of the cherry tree that she wished, but she did not know where the boughs led, or even if they led anywhere at all.

She stood a while in thought, and when that didn't help in the slightest, clutched the enormous watch to her and began to walk along the boughs, looking for a sign or someone to ask; very shortly, she was running as fast as she could along the boughs with the smaller twigs and branches trying to catch in her hair.

She saw no one, not even an insect.

Below her on the ground she saw a hill under the Tree, and a kind of moat that went 'round the hill, and a kind of tangle of green hedges beyond that, and, in the far distance, a beach of white sand in a great ring 'round a large island, and past that, an Ocean that went as far as her eyes could see, with Islands dotting it here and there—some of them seeming to float above the surface of the water, and others to have sunk underneath it.

Whether or not that was all of Wonderland she could not tell.

She ran until she had reached the end of the bough, which split into a vee of two weaker branches, neither of which was strong enough to carry her weight. Then she was forced to turn back around, for she was afraid of falling, and of not knowing where she would land if she did: England, Wonderland, or some other place entirely.

She turned back around and began to walk in the direction of the trunk. "What shall I do, what shall I do?" she asked herself, until she was quite bored of *that*, for no-one gave her an answer.

Finally she was so bored that she began to examine the enormous watch she had been given by the Red Queen, from the Mad Hatter.

When she opened the cover, she sighed: the inside of the watch had been packed with cherry-mash, so that it dripped red juice all over her hands, so that they were even redder than before. It had run down the front of her dress and pinafore as well, making a terrible mess.

As her clothing was already hopelessly dirtied, she pulled up a corner of her pinafore and cleaned the juice off the face of the watch, as best she could.

What was revealed was the oddest watch she had ever seen.

The numerals had been replaced by the phases of the moon. The face of the watch was a moonlit night, with dark sky, bright jeweled stars, and clouds so white they seemed to glow in the twilight. The arms of the watch, one short, one long, were both tipped with silver arrows. Investigating the rest of the watch revealed no instructions, dedications, or maker's mark.

She leaned her ear against the watch's face and heard not the slightest buzz, whirr, or tick.

"Hello," said Alice. "I wonder how this watch works at all, or if it has been stopped by cherry-juice."

"That is a good question," said the Watch, opening one jeweled eye (which Alice had previously assumed to be one of the stars and a cloud moving across the moon).

"Oh!" Alice exclaimed. "I'm terribly sorry. I didn't mean to be rude."

"No offense taken," said the Watch, "unless you were to dip it in chocolate, of which I am quite fond, and then I might reconsider. The offense, that is," the Watch added, in case she hadn't caught its joke.

Alice ignored the Watch's distasteful sense of humor. "I haven't any chocolate," she said.

The Watch sighed and opened another eye. "Butter, perhaps?"

"None of that, either." Alice patted her pockets; all she found were a few arrowroot biscuits that she had been feeding her younger sister, Edith. The Watch accepted them with another sigh, and munched on them contentedly, its cheeks bulging at the half-moons.

"Ah!" it said finally. "One becomes so weary of cherry-juice. And butter."

"Excuse me," Alice said, "could you tell me the way to the Golden Court?"

"The Golden Court!" the Watch said, opening its eyes

quite wide, so wide that Alice could see the gears moving behind the jewels, "You wish to go to the Golden Court?"

"Yes, please," said Alice. "Do you know the way?"

"I am from the Golden Court myself," the Watch said shortly. "I am the Lord of Some-other-time."

Alice put the Watch on the bough and curtseyed to it politely, then picked it up again. "A pleasure to make your acquaintance, your lordship."

"And who are you?" the Watch asked.

"I am Alice—"

The Watch gave a shudder. "*Queen* Alice?"

"I suppose so," Alice said, for she *had* once received a crown in Wonderland, for crossing to the Eighth Square without being captured as a pawn. Or at least she had dreamed that it was so.

"Your Majesty," said the Watch, in a more respectful tone. "I apologize for being forward, but we are in desperate need of your help. I must be returned to the White Rabbit—perhaps you know him—before the sun rises next in Wonderland, or else he shall be executed!"

Alice had a horror of explanations at the best of times, but there was nothing for it but to ask the Watch to explain itself.

"The White Rabbit carries me from the Red Queen's Court to the Golden Court every day at least once, and often twice or more," said the Watch. "Unfortunately, he dropped me just as he was captured by the clerks of the Golden Court, and was forced to leave me behind."

"Why is it so important that the White Rabbit be saved?" she asked.

"He has important information on the Great Unwinding," the Watch said in a hushed tone, looking about him as he did so. "Including who one of the leaders of the rebellion might be!"

"Who is that?"

"I don't know," the Watch admitted. "I was in his pocket at the time, and he and his informant were whispering."

"What is so terrifying about the Great Unwinding anyway?" Alice asked.

"It means that the rebels will destroy the Mainspring, which powers Time itself in Wonderland," the Watch said. "And then…everything will stop!"

Alice blinked in surprise. "For ever?"

"For as long as time can be, without Time," said the Watch. "Although I have heard rumors of a small, hidden spring that could be used for a little while, in order to make repairs on the Mainspring. But that may be nothing more than Golden Court gossip."

Alice chewed on her lip. The situation sounded dire: and besides, she would rather put off reading sermons for as long as was humanly possible.

With great dignity, she said, "I should be delighted to help."

—

The face of the moon continued to watch Alice through the window; it was so full, and so bright, that it was impossible to think of going back to sleep—unless she was dreaming, in which case she already was asleep, and may as well be about the business of her dream.

She swung her legs out of bed and rubbed the sleep out of her eyes without waking Reginald, slipped on a dressing-gown, and went down stairs to the kitchen. She drew herself a cup of cold water and drank it down. The rooms were bright with moonlight; even the ones that did not face the moon seemed to have absorbed it from the air. The rooms were alight with liquid silver.

She stopped in front of the painting of Sunderland that the Reverend Dodgson had given her at her wedding to Reginald. It seemed to be nothing more than a watercolor painting of Tom Quad, at the heart of Christ Church College. She had known the painting for what it was at once, of course: another doorway into Wonderland. He had had it painted while telling a Wonderland story to the artist, he confessed to her in a letter which she had since destroyed, and was giving it to her in case she ever changed her mind and wished to leave England. Wonderland was mad, he admitted, and in the end he had decided against it—but if anyone should be able to leave the ordinary world behind at a moment's notice, it was she, and he had *quite* enough fame, thank you, and no need of writing down another of his Fantasies for the entertainment of, on the whole, some rather stupid people.

It was, she believed, his way of apologizing for all the annoyances that Fame had brought her.

She put her hand on the heavy paper of the painting; as always, it felt warm to the touch and gave slightly under her hand, as though she were pressing flesh, and not fiber and pigment.

The paper began to fold around the sides of her hand. She took her hand away, and brought it back to the sink to wash. Touching the painting always made her feel slightly dirty.

If she pushed harder, her hand would sink into the painting; the deeper it sank, the more the painting would pull on it, until she would have to use all her might to pull herself free—or allow herself to sink into the surface at last.

The Reverend Dodgson had passed two years ago, as had her father—within days of each other, almost like lovers. Alice had three young sons to care for, and a husband who suited her to perfection, even if he was not her first choice (the Queen had prevented *that*).

In short, she was happy. She had no need of Wonderland, and it better not have any need of *her*. She had turned her back on all that long ago, even though, on certain late nights, especially those in which a full moon had risen, she would find herself back in front of the painting, wondering.

To enter Wonderland now, as a grown woman—what would it be like?

Once it had been as easy as falling asleep—or falling down a rabbit-hole—or stepping through a mirror.

Now the way felt like a stranger's flesh, warm and yielding, and the thought of it disgusted her. Her memories of Wonderland had been poisoned over the years. All kinds of foul suggestions and insinuations had made their way to her—all of them perfectly untrue—and no doubt the worst of the worst had been concealed from her, so that she would not have to hear the disgusting words. Charles Dodgson had been a complicated man, one whom she had loved, then pushed aside, then abandoned—but he was *not* what they had accused him of.

And yet—the painting. No one else could feel the paper squirm under their hands but she, not even the children.

Had Reverend Dodgson been poisoned by those words, when he had lived?

Had Wonderland?

The Watch, despite its initial claims, did *not* know the way to the Golden Court, having been kept inside the White Rabbit's vest-pocket most of the time (how this should be so, Alice did not know, because the Watch was so large that she had to hold it in both arms, like a baby), but it *did* know one thing.

"You must start at nine o'clock," said the Watch.

"What time is it now?" Alice inquired.

"Why, it is Some-other-time," said the Watch, with some aspersion. "We are at the center peg that holds it all together—that is, it isn't any particular time at all. A time for putting things off another day. A time which, by the way, has come to an end."

This did not sound like the sort of time that Alice was used to, not at all. She chewed the inside of her cheek, thinking with furious haste. "If it is Some-other-time, then…which way shall I go for nine o'clock?"

The two hands on the clock face swung to the left-hand side of the dial. Alice turned slowly, and the two hands remained pointing in the same direction, which happened to be toward the end of a long cherry-bough. "And what direction is that?" Alice asked.

"North is six, South is three, West is twelve, and the rest should be obvious," the Watch said.

But Alice had learnt that nothing in Wonderland was obvious, and so she asked again: "And so this is East? Is that correct?"

The Watch snorted, rolling its jeweled eyes. "East, nine o'clock, next Sunday!" it exclaimed. "What does it matter, they're all the same direction! Go that way, and hurry!"

Alice proceeded along the bough, walking among the leaves hanging down around her, holding the Watch in front of her to make sure the hands stayed pointing in the same direction, which was marked on the dial with the waning half-moon.

"Can one only walk to next Sunday from here?" she asked. "Mightn't one walk to, oh, last month, if one knew its direction?"

"Don't be ridiculous," answered the Watch. "One simply cannot put something off until almost the last moment, if one has already done it a month ago. One would have to go through all sorts of mazes and confusions, to come to last month!"

"Ah," said Alice, as though the Watch's answer had revealed anything of sense at all.

They were very quickly reaching the end of the bough, until finally there was no more wood in front of her. The hands on the face of the Watch still pointed in the same direction.

"Hurry, hurry," cried the Watch.

"But there is no more branch," answered Alice.

"Of course there is!"

Alice looked down at the distant ground underneath her and sighed, then took a step forward. No matter what happened to her next, it was still better than sermons.

Instead of falling, she was swung violently about, so that her foot struck the wood of the branch that had been below and now was above her.

With hardly a hitch in her stride she kept walking forward along the underside of the branch. She did not *feel* upside down, which was lucky, or she soon would have been ill.

"Hurry, hurry!" the Watch cried. "It has been put off for far too long! We must reach next Sunday before dawn!"

—

The Master Chronometer is nearly as large as Wonderland itself, being on the opposite side of the island upon which the daylit Wonderland rests; it appears to be an enormous plate of polished brass upon which rest many gears, screws, escapements, springs, bridges, balancing wheels, regulators, and jewels the color of cherries—rubies, which are used to decrease friction along the bearings.

The heart of the Master Chronometer is the Mainspring, which is separated from the rest of the Master Chronometer by a canyon or chasm, across which four bridges span, one for each of the cardinal directions. The Mainspring itself rests inside an enormous, flat barrel the size of a small city. The barrel is topped with the clearest crystal, so that one might see inside to the four great shimmering wires, no thicker than a hair and as long as Time itself. Within the barrel are also, if one has the patience and discipline to watch for them, the tiny bronze fleas who oil and tend and watch the breath of the Mainspring—and who have been sealed up in the barrel with it since the beginning of Wonderland itself, living and dying and repairing each other across innumerable generations.

The Central Palace, which occupies the center of the Mainspring and rises up into a needlelike tower stretching into the heavens, is an edifice so elegant that one might think it made out of lace, or snowflakes. But it is all metal, all springs and delicate gears slowly turning, so slowly that eons might pass with only a single tick. It glimmers in the moonlight shining over the Chronometer, like a silver arabesque decorated with deep red jewels.

At first, the Master Chronometer is a deafening place, and one's first instinct is to put one's hands over one's ears; however, the sound produced is such that trying to shut it out is impossible, as the entire plate upon which the Chronometer is built vibrates with the ticking and turning of the various parts of the great watch. By turns, one becomes inured to the sound. One hears it no more than one hears the beating of one's heart.

The daylit Wonderlandians, when first they arrive in the vast city that is the Master Chronometer itself, each suffer a small moment of terror and dizziness, in which they are both deafened and afraid. But soon they recover, and step upon their treadmills, or grasp their handles, and begin their work. When all the daylit Wonderlandians are working, the sound of their movements is a soothing sound, a whisper that makes the rest of the sounds of the clock sound natural, the workings of a body at rest, a soft purr that lulls one almost to sleep.

Alice followed the underside of the branch to the trunk, and found there a staircase cunningly hidden on the undersides of the boughs as they joined the cherry-tree trunk. What seemed from above a bulge in the bark here or there, from below, was revealed as well-made stair-steps, upon which one might skip as easily as one pleased. When right-side up, she never would have noticed them, but now she followed them under branch and bole until finally she arrived at a small, narrow hole in the trunk, leading inside the tree itself.

"Ah! We will soon be making some progress now," said the Watch, with some satisfaction.

Alice shifted the Watch over to one hip, as if it were some sort of small child, and patted all around the hole. It was slim, only two feet in width at the widest part, but she was still able to slide through it by first pushing the Watch gingerly through, then edging sideways herself.

When Alice had picked the Watch up again, it remarked, "We are almost past nine o'clock, and will have to change Time soon."

Alice did not have a moment to ask him what he meant, for suddenly the crack in the trunk closed up behind her with a thump!

"Oh!" she cried.

"Don't drop me!" cried the Watch.

"But I can't see!"

The face of the Watch began to glow dimly in the darkness of the trunk. By its light, she could see that the hands had changed: now they pointed toward the half-moon.

"North!" declared the Watch. "*Now* we're heading somewhere important! Winter! And Six! And Yesterday!"

"Are we much closer, then?" asked Alice.

"Oh, we haven't even begun," said the Watch. "Hurray,

hurray! For it is Winter! And Yesterday." It gave another tug in her hand, leading her straight into the wooden heart of the trunk.

She stumbled along after it, expecting to feel the thump of the cherry-tree's heartwood against her nose. She closed her eyes. "You really ought to be more…"

She was about to say *careful*, but was interrupted by a cold wind blowing all 'round her.

She opened her eyes. It may or may not have been Yesterday…but it was indisputable that they had arrived in Winter.

PART II – SIX O'CLOCK – NORTH – WINTER – 'ROUND AND 'ROUND – YESTERDAY

For the first two times Alice Pleasance Hargreaves had been to Wonderland, she had gone away and arrived back in the real world after nothing more the length of a pleasant nap. She would have thought the two journeys nothing but a dream—except for one thing: that the Reverend Dodgson knew of her adventures without her having to tell him.

He added to them and embellished them, so realistically that she was sometimes unsure which parts she had actually dreamed. At the time she had been quite annoyed: was he stealing her dream, or was she stealing his? In either case, he could at least do her the courtesy of recording the theft accurately.

And now?

Now she would never know, would she? For Reverend Dodgson was dead, and had not written down whatever story lay in wait for her on the other side of the painting. She would have to dream her dream, and guess whether he had known it before she did.

Or was it, after all this time, simply too late?

To go through the painting now, or to wait? For she *would* go through sooner or later, even if it made her mad, or killed her, or made her go out, *bang*, like the Reverend Dodgson's proverbial candle—all hope of Heaven simply extinguished.

Motherhood and marriage to Reginald had made her more sensible than she had been as a girl, but had not entirely snuffed out the compulsions of curiosity.

If she did *not* go, she would go mad of it, or become so dull that she would forget what madness was entirely. That she knew for certain.

Winter was a proper garden, filled with trimmed hedges whose leaves had fallen but which remained tightly woven, so that to try to push between them was to invite a terrible tangle of clothing and hair, and no guarantee of getting through, no matter how hard one tried.

Alice and the Watch (who was, fortunately, warm enough to keep Alice's teeth from chattering) had appeared on the little hill overlooking the garden, and which surrounded the enormous cherry tree. The moat that surrounded the hill appeared to be not at all frozen, although the climb down to the water was quite steep, and she did not know how she would get back out again. Instead she crossed on the bridge nearest her; it appeared to be made of cherry-tree roots that had been trained to grow across.

The moon still hung overhead, but had gone from a half-moon to a full one, making the snow almost blindingly bright.

"Like explorers of the Northwest Passage," Alice said, "We should have brought a balaclava, for now I shall be soon blinded."

"Nonsense," said the Watch. "Forward! Onward! Six o'clock sha'n't last long! And then where shall we be, lost in the mazes of Winter forever, until I wind down and you freeze to death? The beetles shall rescue me and take me to the Golden Court, although I shall have to be fined if they do, but you will be left standing here, like a pitiable statue!"

Alice hefted the Watch onto one hip and shaded her eyes. The garden did seem to be a maze, with its tall hedges blocking the route this way and that.

She tilted the Watch so she could see its face. "Where are we going? For it seems as though the garden goes on forever."

"It only *seems* that way," said the Watch. "Really it's not very big at all. Unless one becomes lost, of course, in which case the garden is *very* large indeed."

"How shall we know which way to go?"

The eyes of the Watch blinked at her, turning back into moonlit clouds for a moment. "How shall we know which way to go? Why, we shall always walk in the direction of six o'clock, of course."

Alice sighed. To the Watch, such a thing might seem simple, but that was because it was a Watch, used to being carried about.

The hands of the Watch were pointed at six o'clock, or straight toward Alice. No matter which direction she turned, the hands pointed in the same direction. And when she took a step forward, the Watch screeched in rage: "Six o'clock! Six o'clock! Are you deaf? Are you quite stupid? Oh, what a misfortune it is, to have to be carried by such a girl as you!"

Having tried every other direction, Alice brushed the frost off her cheeks (for it was very cold), straightened up, and proceeded to walk backward instead of forward.

"That's it, that's it," said the Watch encouragingly.

It *might* have explained itself better, thought Alice.

Walking backwards without falling down in the thin, icy snow that lay before the first row of hedges was not easy, but the distance passed quickly, so quickly that wind ruffled through her hair. The first row of hedges rushed past her, then swung about sharply—without her meaning to, her feet had turned to follow the path underneath them.

She tried to twist her head 'round to see what was behind her—she didn't like the idea of banging into one of the hedges or a fountain, let alone one of the hedge-animals—

but the Watch screamed, "Don't look back! Don't look backwards when you're in Yesterday!"

But the Watch's warning was a moment too late.

An old woman sat in a library lined with books, watching Alice intently. Her wrinkled old hands lay in her lap, and she wore a dingy, worn dress trimmed with lace, as well as a felt hat with a feather in it. The woman had become quite stout around the middle, and her wizened, half-lidded eyes seemed to have no expression in them whatsoever.

She looked *terribly* dull.

Alice shuddered and turned her head the other direction immediately, for she recognized the woman as herself, grown quite old.

"Never look back when you're in Yesterday," the Watch announced. "For one only sees Tomorrow, and Tomorrow is an unpleasant place, full of—"

"Oh, do stop explaining," Alice cried, hugging the Watch to her chest. "Hush, hush!"

She kept walking, and the maze of hedges swung 'round again and again. She did not dare to look over her shoulder.

"Steady, steady," said the Watch. "Slower…and now stop!"

Her feet carried her past a frozen fountain, beside which sat a beautiful woman who was peering down at herself.

At first, Alice thought she was frozen, but then the woman looked up.

"Mother?"

—

They had called Lorina Hanna Liddell (née Reeve) the Kingfisher, for she was so intent on getting royal (or at least noble) husbands for her daughters, that she had lost all common decency in the matter. She had married up in status, to Henry George Liddell, who became Vice-Chancellor of Oxford University, and who had published (with Robert Scott), *A Greek-English Lexicon* in 1843, which was still in use over fifty years later.

Other people called her less flattering things, and it was an open secret that Charles Dodgson had mocked her by making a caricature of her in *Alice's Adventures in Wonderland*, after which she had forced him to break with the family. The truth had been fogged over by the various rumors, for example, that the Reverend Dodgson was in love with Mrs. Liddell, or else her daughter Ina, or else Alice, or else the governess, Miss Pritchett, when in reality it was simply that he had told jokes that Mrs. Liddell did not understand, but that her husband laughed richly and merrily at; he had spent too much time with the girls telling them stories, or with her husband, discussing the Greek that she would never read; and then had the audacity to disagree with her husband over matters at Christ Church College, where Henry had been Dean at the time; and so Reverend Dodgson was found to be intolerable and interfering, a detriment to the characters of youth, putting ideas in the heads of her daughters as well as the students over whom Henry had been raised.

And so Reverend Dodgson must go, for one reason or another, and if some of the rumors hazing over the truth should be traced back to Mrs. Liddell, well, she would know, wouldn't she?

Alice had been the child who had come closest to accomplishing Mrs. Liddell's fondest wish, for she had been in love with the youngest son of Queen Victoria, Prince Leopold, but the queen had always wished for Leopold to wed the child of one of the other Protestant monarchies, she didn't much care which, and so he was united with Princess Helene Friederike of Waldeck-Pyrmont of the German Empire.

The fact that it had been her most rebellious, least-liked child who had come the closest, did not much matter to Mrs. Liddell.

There was nothing for it, Alice finally decided. Grown woman or not, she *would* go to Wonderland, and face whatever the Reverend Dodgson had left behind for her, or discover that there was nothing left to be found.

If something happened to her, well, the boys were old enough to be without their mother, if they must. They had a good governess who was fond of them, and a father who would love them in the rough-and-tumble way that they so adored.

She could not linger on this threshold forever; she must go through, or else curiosity would murder all good feeling.

Tonight…tonight.

It must be tonight. Some decisions must not be put off, once they have been made, or else the soul would wither.

Should she remove the painting from the wall, so that she might climb through it more easily? She grasped the edges of the frame to lift it, then changed her mind. She was only making another delay; she knew very well that it did not need to be done.

She pushed her hand into the painting. It sank past the surface of the paper, into the warmth and smoothness of flesh. She pushed her hand further inside; the flesh tightened against her hand for a moment, the way a horse's flank will twitch when a fly lands on it, then gave and stretched, allowing her to sink deeper in.

She pushed until she was as far in as her arm would go, then ducked her head into the frame, hooked the other arm inside it as well, and pulled herself in.

The woman beside the fountain, her face and hair and clothing covered in frost, blinked slowly at Alice. "Whoever might you be?" she asked in a slow, ponderous manner.

Alice almost burst out with, "Why, I am your daughter Alice," but stopped herself just in time, for it seemed as though there were something the matter with her mother: the expressions of her face and the sound of her voice both seemed somewhat foreign to Alice, as if they possessed the slightest echo. Her skin glistened in the moonlight.

Why had her mother come to Wonderland? It was most unusual of her mother to do anything the slightest bit nonsensical at all.

Alice bit her lip and waited for her mother to speak.

"There, there," whispered the Watch. "It will have always been all right, you'll see. This is Winter…six o'clock…yesterday…"

Its voice faded into silence.

"You look terribly familiar," her mother said, slowly getting to her feet from where she had been kneeling next to the fountain, to look into its frozen waters. "I'm sure I've seen you before."

Alice shook her head and gave the best curtsy she could, with the Watch in her arms as it was. "I've only just arrived in Wonderland, mum," she said.

Her mother pulled her hand free of the icy stone, and a layer of ice crackled and sprang off her hand, showering fragments on the flagstones. "And yet you remind me of someone…"

Alice's mouth began to gape at the sight of hard-frozen ice breaking off from her mother's skin, as though her mother hadn't the slightest amount of warmth to her.

Her mother's dress, which was not heavy enough for the cold, began to scatter ice chips as well; the more her mother moved, the more it seemed that she had been frozen up in the ice. She pulled one foot off the ground with a tearing sound, then the other.

And that was not the worst of it: for Alice had noticed that on the back of her mother's hand, more than just a patch of ice had crackled and come loose, but part of the pale white skin of her mother's hand. Underneath was a glimmer of brass or some other shiny metal.

Alice backed away from her, rather hoping that she would soon be carried out of arm's reach by the powerful workings of the Watch.

However, it was only an ordinary step that she took. She did not go zooming through the garden paths, only pressed directly backward into the hedge, with little prickles of branch and thorn against her back.

Alice's breath came out of her in great heaving puffs. Her mother's breath did not warm the air at all.

More of the skin flaked away from her mother's hand in a long dry patch that crumbled up her arm, taking skin and flesh and sleeve with them as they fell, all in pieces. Underneath the skin were gears and rods and wires and metal joints, the kind that one might find in a clockwork toy.

The creature that walked toward her was *not* her mother, but some sort of automaton.

Alice backed away from it.

"Aren't all the Wonderlandians supposed to be in the Golden Court, winding the Master Chronometer?" she hissed at the Watch.

"Winter is one of the outlying courts," whispered the Watch. "Perhaps she serves as a guardian?"

The creature lurched closer and closer, raising its cold, white hands toward Alice as it came.

Alice shook her head again and again, raising the Watch as a shield between them. "You are not *my mother*," she cried. "You are only a figment!"

"A figment? What does that mean?" the thing that was not her mother asked.

"A paint made out of figs," Alice replied immediately. "All the photographers use them now, to add the color to their silver plates; otherwise, you wouldn't be able to see the pictures that they take, for they would be all in silver, silver shadows under a silver moon. And they wouldn't be half so…so tasty!"

Fortunately the automaton had no sense of humor, and didn't understand a word of the nonsense Alice was saying. It frowned, and the strain of frowning caused the corners of her mouth to crumble, showing more brass gears moving underneath. "But isn't that what's called a fragment?"

"No, no, a fragment is a woody green bush that only grows on islands, whose leaves possess a curious flavor that goes well with lamb!"

The automaton's hands finally reached the Watch, and it began to try to pull the Watch away from Alice. She clung to it as hard as she could; the automaton's hands clawed at her arm, leaving stinging scratches.

"Ow!"

Alice clung even tighter to the Watch, but it began to slip from her grasp.

"A shipment?" asked the automaton as its face sloughed

off completely, leaving behind a metal plate filled with gears and escapements, whirring springs, jeweled eyes… "An infant? An instant?"

"Don't let go!" the Watch shrieked. "Oh, Alice! Oh! Oh! Oh!"

Suddenly the Watch slid out of Alice's arms and was flung beyond the automaton and into the hedges of the maze.

"A signet? A piglet? A garment? A magnet? A pageant? A patent?" said the automaton. Now that the Watch was no longer between them, its hands, now nothing but jointed brass claws, reached for Alice's throat.

"A rabbit?"

"Yes, yes!" cried Alice, as the horrible fingers closed around her throat. "A rabbit! We are looking for a—"

She could speak no more, for the metallic hands had closed too tight. And then she fell down *another* rabbit hole, as the edges of her world went gray.

At first Alice Hargreaves saw only darkness on the other side of the picture-frame, and her heart sank: Wonderland had ended, and there was left only this, a formless nothingness.

Then she shook off her mood and stood up, for she had always been a practical woman—in her own way.

She had landed or climbed out onto a pile of leaves, only slightly damp and moldy-smelling. When she stood, she was able to see over the top of a ridge or pile of dirt that was mounded up on one side of the hole, and glimpse a spot of daylight: it was only her eyes adjusting from the bright moonlight that had made it seem so impossibly dark.

"Rabbit?" she called. "Hello? Anyone?"

It was a familiar place, although she had only ever glimpsed it briefly—the hole through which she had fallen as a girl, when the White Rabbit had led her down into Wonderland. Far, far above her was a pinprick of light, so dim that she could only see it if she looked very slightly away from it, out of the corner of her eye.

She suspected that her childhood, her *real* one, might be far above her—waiting for her to climb back up the tunnel and emerge into the past.

For a moment she was tempted to climb, to do it all over again, this time with the benefit of hindsight.

But no; she had lived that time once, and endured its joys and sorrows. To relive it and try to perfect it would increase the sorrows—and make the joys puff into thin air.

She shook the leaves out of her dressing-gown and patted her hair, which was still pulled into a thick, brown braid that flowed almost to her waist. She was barefoot, which she now regretted; it would only have taken a few minutes to have put slippers on before she had gone through the painting—!

But now, of course, it was too late.

She climbed over the mound of dirt, taking care to keep her dressing gown as clean as possible, and entered the tunnel beyond. It quickly turned from a hole in the dirt to one of the long corridors of Christ Church, where her father had for so long been the Dean.

It came to an abrupt end in a small hall surrounded with doors. It almost reminded her of one of the common rooms, although she did not quite recognize it. The door she entered through closed behind her, and once it had, the room swam around her, and she was unable of course to tell which of the doors she had entered through. Each of the doors were identical—and they seemed to squirm about as she looked at them, so that she could not tell even how many of them there were.

She waited for the little door leading to the garden, and the table, and the key, and the little bottle marked "Drink Me" to appear.

This time it would be easier; this time she would get it right.

A lice awoke from the automaton's terrible strangulation neither dead nor in the garden: she was underneath the surface of a deep pool with light glimmering far above her on the surface.

She felt not the slightest bit of fear while floating underneath the waves, even though she was quite unable to breathe. She was rising slowly, her arms and legs outspread. The water felt light, even though it surrounded her completely. It rushed between her fingers, it unwound her hair and made it stream out behind her wildly, it caught in the ribbons of her pinafore and tugged playfully on them.

She rose, but in which direction—next Sunday—Yesterday—or what other time—she had no idea.

The White Rabbit patted its waistcoat-pocket, but of course it was empty; his Watch had been lost when he had been arrested. The moon had almost reached its zenith, and no sign of Alice, the Watch, or any other form of salvation in sight.

With still so much to do! He had finally convinced the Red Queen and the Crown of the plot against the Mainspring—his informant, the Hatter, had been *most* convincing—and now it but remained to identify the ringleaders, stop them, and repair the Mainspring so that this sort of thing was unlikely to happen again.

He sighed.

The White Rabbit had been placed in a cell toward the top of the needle-like Center Palace tower; the walls, ceiling, and even floor of his cell all turned, so that it was impossible to stand still for any length of time. If he did not continue hopping about here and there, he would be pushed off the spokes and ground between the gears and plates underfoot.

There was no bed or chair, no place to rest. His "cell" was in reality a torture-chamber.

Sooner or later he must sleep, whether he wanted to or

not. He had taught himself to get by without much of it—the Watch had kept him from having to be transported at moonrise to the Great Chronometer for the nightly work, but he would still have to go, when he slept—but to endure without any sleep at all —?

He would lapse, and fall, and be ground up in the gears.

And if that weren't enough torture, then there was also the thinnest of opportunities to escape offered him by the movement of the prison. Once every hour, the gears making up the walls turned so that there was a moment in which he might—if he were clever and quick—be able to leap out of his prison.

It would be a bit of a scrape, even if he timed it perfectly. If he approached it wrongly, then he would likewise lose a foot, an ear—his head! He sighed, and shifted from the spoke of one gear to another, and then onto a third.

His imprisonment was the least of his worries.

For he had learnt another terrible fact about Wonderland: it was unnecessary for the daylit Wonderlandians to be slaves to the Great Chronometer every night.

The last thing he had tried to do in the Red Queen's court before he had been arrested, was to try to explain this to her. She had waved him off. "I hate explanations!" she had said. "Off with you!"

And rather than have his head off as well, he had left off his explaining and fled.

But the truth was this: the work done by the Wonderlandians

to wind the Mainspring was less than the winding they received at the end of every night in return. The daylit Wonderlandians would frolic all throughout the daylit hours, doing no work, and then work all night—their lives were half work, and half play.

But if that were all the winding that the Mainspring received, then it should have unwound a long time ago! For even the sun and the moon were made of clockwork, and driven by the Mainspring. Who wound *them*?

Additionally, the moonlit Wonderlandians did not work during the daylit hours; they were instead conscripted to become additional gears of the Great Chronometer, the parts that created the illusion of the semblance of life and flesh.

Who provided the winding that wound them?

No, the Mainspring must be wound some other way.

The Hatter had whispered that the conspirators of the Great Unwinding spoke of a mysterious personage, the Watchmaker, who had both made the Master Chronometer and who wound it in secret to this day.

However, this Watchmaker, *if* he existed, was failing. The Mainspring had long been losing tension; soon it would not have the energy to drive the gears that rewound both the daylit and moonlit Wonderlandians, and then what would happen?

The White Rabbit was but a messenger; he did not know.

And now someone in the Golden Court had ordered him arrested—and here he was, unable to tell anyone what he had learnt from the Hatter, not even a guard—for the cell itself was his guard.

The White Rabbit shook his head as a bell began to toll the hour of Six.

The walls of the cell were coming into position now. In a moment the spokes of the gears would align, leaving a narrow, brief passage out of his cell.

If he managed to escape, he would surely be recaptured almost immediately and put back into his cell.

He slipped out of his waistcoat and dropped it onto the floor, where it began to drag underfoot as the gears caught it. Then he hopped from one spoke to another, then a third, waiting for the right moment.

If nothing else, he might be able to catch forty winks before they tossed him back into this mechanical torture device.

The gears lined up, providing a slim window of opportunity.

He jumped.

One of the doors in the little hall opened, and Alice Hargreaves ran over and stuck her bare foot into it promptly. She was a grown woman and could handle the pain of a few pinched toes now and then.

Through the door was a garden, very neatly laid out with a complex hedge-maze, at the bottom of a hill and across a little moat or stream (a sturdy stone bridge arched over it, quite picturesquely). Fountains and hedge-animals rested in the center of little clearings between the hedges, which had grown very tall but remained tidy and trimmed. Bright flowers spilled over vases and flower-boxes and from flower-beds throughout the maze, with many pinks and oranges and purples. The hum of bees hung contentedly in the air.

It was pretty, and very similar to the garden that she had tried so hard to reach the first time she had come to Wonderland, but was it what she wanted, where she would like to go? It was impossible to know, without more information.

To go through the door simply because it was there—or simply because it was the only choice offered—or simply because she was bored—was a childish thing to do.

Leaving her foot wedged between doorframe and heavy old door, Alice looked back into the hall behind her.

A little table had appeared, and on top of it was a small damask-velvet notebook and a golden key.

On the notebook was a tag, and on the tag—it was lit from above, as if by moonlight—were the words *Read Me*.

Alice ground her teeth together.

The late Reverend Dodgson had been many things, but he had not been stupid. He knew what tempted her now that she was grown was *an explanation*.

If she took her foot out of the doorway, it would close itself and lock—and the key might not be for the same doorway, or any doorway at all.

If she went through the doorway, it would close itself

and lock as well—and then she would be unable to get the notebook, and satisfy her curiosity.

There was nothing else within her reach that she could use to wedge in the doorway.

Damned if she did, damned if she didn't. The tyranny of paradox.

The door squeezed against her foot, as if to remind her that she was wasting time.

Alice squared her shoulders, took a deep breath, then—flung open the door and went through it.

Not only did it slam and lock behind her (she could hear a key turning in the lock, as if some invisible creature had been standing next to her, waiting for her to make her choice, in the little hall), but when she looked back over her shoulder, it had disappeared. She was standing at the top of a hill underneath an enormous, spreading cherry-tree. The garden remained where it was, across the bridge at the bottom of the hill.

However, no entrance into the hedge-maze across the stream was to be seen, even when Alice walked all 'round the base of the tree. No way in, and no way out.

One direction seeming much like any other, Alice chose a direction and walked toward it, crossing the bridge at the base of the hill. The grass lay softly underfoot, the breeze fluttered with the leaves flirtatiously, and, as she approached, the hedge opened up in front of her in an archway, revealing another line of hedge.

Alice held her arms out from her sides to keep from getting crushed, in case the hedge decided to change its mind. She *would* go through.

Alice had floated to the surface and was considering whether to stay in the pleasant water or to attempt to swim to land, when an enormous hand reached down to her. Out of curiosity, she reached up to touch it; her own, minuscule hand became suddenly larger, and was able to clasp the one held out to her.

It pulled firmly on her own, lifting her out of the water.

Breaking through the surface of the water felt exactly like going through a mirror, at least in Alice's limited experience. At any rate it was a curious sensation. Then her head was breaking through, and she was lifted bodily out of the water and stood upon the edge of a marble fountain.

She was perfectly dry, and only slightly chilled. It was still Winter, after all, with the wind whispering through the last few leaves in the hedges, and ice underfoot.

The fountain was a large white marble one, with four mermaids drinking tea and gossiping with each other, and a society lady in the center, pouring a frozen arc of ice out of a teapot. The surface of the fountain had frozen solid, and shown no sign of having been disturbed by her coming out of it.

The person who had pulled her out of it was the Reverend Dodgson.

"Hello, Alice," he said. "Has your dunking quite dried you off?"

It had; a little shake of her head told her that her hair wasn't the slightest bit heavy or damp. "It has, thank you."

"I thought it might."

She frowned at him. "What are you doing here, Reverend Dodgson?" she asked.

"Why, rescuing you."

"From what?"

"From the piece of clockwork posing as your mother."

She gave him a little curtsy on the edge of the fountain. "Thank you."

He had wrinkles on his face, not deep ones but wrinkles all the same, and liver-spots on his hands. His lips seemed to have curled in on themselves with the corners turned down, so that he was perpetually frowning.

"Have you been sad?" she asked.

"Oh, yes, very sad," he said.

"For a long time? Your face shows it."

He took her under the arms and set her off the edge of the fountain onto the frozen grass. "Let us not talk any longer of sadness," he said. "Instead, let us walk through this pleasant garden, and talk of summer things."

"But it is Winter," Alice said.

His thin, nearly-white eyebrows beetled together. "Winter? But it is summer now. July the fourth, as a matter of fact, the same day that I told you and your sisters—"

"Then why is the fountain frozen, and the grass covered in frost, and the leaves all fallen?"

He frowned at the little clearing in the garden, shook his head, and sighed. "It seems just a moment ago that it was Summer. I have been snubbed by Time, you see. She and I used to linger together, but now she will not see me, and passes me by."

Alice, being used to the Reverend Dodgson's mysterious pronouncements, only said, "Do you know the way to the Golden Court?"

"The Golden Court!" he said. "The place where the Great Chronometer keeps track of all the time of Wonderland, and all the money, too."

"The White Rabbit is about to be executed for not paying his time properly, or some such thing," Alice agreed. "I have been sent to rescue him by the Red Queen."

The two of them had begun to walk around the fountain, first clockwise, then counter-clockwise, and then back again. As they walked, Alice noticed that the mermaids at each corner of the fountain were holding cups with cracks in them, so that even if the fountain were working and they managed to catch the water, it would soon run out again.

"How did you come to find the Garden?" Reverend Dodgson asked.

"Why, I was given the White Rabbit's Pocket Watch by the Red Queen," said Alice. "And it gave me directions. It pulled me this way, then that—it told me which way to go—it led me to the underside of the branch of the cherry tree—and then into the trunk—and then into the Winter garden—"

"And where is it now?"

"It was taken from me by the automaton that looked like my mother, and thrown into a hedge, where it disappeared," she said.

"How will you know what direction to go, without it?"

She lifted her chin. "If *you* do not know, then I shall go in the direction of six o'clock until I cannot go that direction any longer, and then I shall see."

"What shall you see?"

"Whatever there is to see. I hope by then to be able to see the Golden Court, and be able to make my way directly there."

"Oh, the ways in Wonderland are never direct," said Reverend Dodgson. "One would think you would know that by now, Alice."

The grass under Alice Hargreaves's feet was warm, the sunlight bright, the day inviting—the kind of summer day that called for a picnic-basket and a story.

She might be inside a story but, alas, could find not the slightest sign of a luncheon.

She wandered the hedge maze. To the right, then forward, then left, then left again, then right—then there was a branching that she followed to the left—then forward, then a place where several hedges ran parallel to each other briefly, a leafy green wall blocking the ends of each with no way to know whether they ran right or left or ended abruptly, and she took the middle of the three, then to the left again, then right.

Then she walked into a clearing with a white marble fountain in the center, where four stonework mermaids were being served tea by a stonework lady in proper dress in the latest style—this despite the fact that the faces of the mermaids as well as the tips of their tails seemed somewhat worn, as if they had rested within this garden for centuries.

As for the lady, Alice had a dress that was almost exactly the same—a lace-trimmed blouse with an elaborate buttoned front, a skirt with a tiny waist that flounced out into a long skirt with three smart tiers of cloth—*not* ruffles—at the bottom.

As for the mermaids, they had crowns of roses in their hair, nude bosoms, and serene yet vain faces. Each statue was probably titled something trite at the bottom, like "Vanity" or "Old Age" or "Society," and was supposed to show how one could pour and pour, and still never fill the cups—which were all cracked.

Dull and moral. She had seen its kind before.

The little clearing in which the fountain played was empty but for a brass pocket-watch that lay on the flagstones surrounding the fountain. She bent down to pick it up.

The cover was open; the face of the pocket-watch was decorated with a sunlit sky sprinkled with clouds. A small circle with the face of an infant lay at noon; a small child's lay at three, a young woman's at six, and an old woman's at nine. The two hands pointed toward six o'clock for a moment, but then both hands shifted toward three o'clock as she watched.

She turned over the watch and tried to pry open the back—

"Enough!" cried a tiny voice.

She turned the Watch over; several of the clouds had split open, revealing brass gears and angry red jewel bearings within: the Watch appeared to have grown a face, consisting of two eyes and a small, rounded mouth shaped like an O.

It looked deeply offended. Alice smiled.

"I'm sorry?" she asked. "Enough of what?"

"Enough poking and prodding and prying!" cried the Watch.

Alice tapped on the glass face of the Watch with her fingernail. "Is it? You don't seem to be working properly." For the hands of the watch had shifted from three—the small child—to the face of the baby, noon. "Perhaps if I pull you apart and check to make sure your gears are clean…?"

"No!" the Watch shouted. "I am working exactly the way I should. I am a Wonderlandian Watch. I do not measure such a simple thing as the position of the *sun*," it added, with contempt.

"What do you measure then, the stages of life?"

"I measure Time," announced the watch, pompously.

Alice tucked her dressing gown underneath her and sat on the edge of the fountain. The Watch didn't have a chain or a loop, and its crown was so recessed that she couldn't have turned it with her fingernails.

She tilted it in the sunlight, throwing reflections from the glass into the water.

"You needn't sit so close to the edge!" the watch cried.

"Oh? Why is that?"

"Because you might drop me in the water, and then I would be ruined!"

"Would you?" she asked.

"I would!"

"I once knew a watch that could keep the time from passing tea-time all day," she said. "No matter what it had been dropped in. Butter, tea—"

"I am not that watch! I am not that watch!"

"Oh? Which watch are you?"

She hadn't moved off the edge of the fountain; when the Watch didn't answer, she shifted her weight slightly toward the waves and stretched out her arm, as if using the glass face to check her appearance. The lady pouring out the tea was circling back around, and almost about to splash water onto the case.

The Watch shrieked in terror. "I belong to the White Rabbit!"

"Mmmmm," said Alice. "I think not. You haven't a pocket-chain, nor a place to put one, and if I remember the White Rabbit, and I do, then he was a Rabbit fond of gold watch-chain charms, and never would have taken a simple watch such as yourself when a more ostentatious one would do."

The Watch did not answer.

Alice merely waited: the tea-pouring woman pouring her tea closer and closer.

Wonderlandians were never as trifling and innocent as they seemed to be—but then, neither was she.

The water splashed closer…closer still…

"I'll talk!" cried the Watch.

She didn't move—it was only testing her nerve.

"I belong to the Great Chronometer!" it shrieked.

She waited. The first droplets of water were splashing on her hand now. One of them landed on the glass face of the Watch.

"You heartless worm!" the Watch cried. "I'll have you fed to the birds!"

Still, she didn't move. The water began to run over the back of her hand.

For an instant, she glanced upward, and met the hollow stone pupils of the woman at the center of the fountain: each woman's eyes seemed to fasten upon the other's, and both their lips seemed to twitch ever so slightly upward.

The Watch, finally, broke.

"I belong to the Great Unwinding! I hope you tick for all eternity!" It proceeded to curse at her in strange terms:

"You over-tightened winding pin! You twisted spring! You...you bent-toothed gear!"

Alice carefully kept the Watch just at the edge of the water for a moment longer, and it obliged with a steady stream of invective. "Your bearings are filled with muck! Your escapement is loose! Your face is scratched and your hands twitch on the hour! *You are always five minutes late!*"

Finally Alice couldn't keep a straight face any longer, and pulled the Watch away from the stream of fountain-water. She clucked her tongue at it. "There, there. You're upset. You should take a moment to calm yourself."

The Watch began to tick louder, and slightly faster— "You'll run yourself ahead, I swear," Alice noted.

The hands spun around the dial twice, then stopped at noon for a moment as the Watch scowled at her. Then it closed its eyes and the hands sank in either direction, toward three and nine, then to six, dangling limply at the bottom of the face.

"Very well," it said. "You win. You have caught me. I do not belong to the White Rabbit...but you have, indeed, seen me before, for once I belonged to the Mad Hatter, and his terrible companion, the March Hare."

"Ahhhh," Alice said. "I can't say that I recognize you; when I saw you, your face—"

"Was completely covered in butter," the Watch snarled angrily.

"And now?" said Alice. "You belong to the Great Unwinding. What, pray tell, is that?"

The hands raised slightly—to about five and seven—then sank back down again. "You won't like it," it warned. "Unless you are made of clockwork…you could never understand."

"Tell me," she urged it. She could just see the eye of the lady pouring tea out of the corner of her eye; it seemed to urge her to encourage confidences. "I shall do my best."

"The Great Unwinding," said the Watch, then stopped. For a moment Alice wondered if she were going to have to terrify it again, but before she could make up her mind to do so, it said, "Wonderland is mad, it is driven by madness, madness is what makes it tick, from top to bottom. Did you know that?"

"I had some suspicion," Alice said drily.

The watch closed its eyes and twitched slightly in Alice's hand, so that it was facing upward, toward the sun.

"The Mainspring must be replaced," said the watch.

"Your mainspring?" Alice asked, although the way the Watch had said the word gave it an almost sacred undertone.

"*The* Mainspring," the Watch said. "The Mainspring that drives all of Wonderland. Everything that comes from Wonderland is made of clockwork, that must be wound up night by night, or else it will run down, and then we will be no more—or if we are, we will not know it, for we sha'n't have any thoughts to know it with."

"You don't look like clockwork," said Alice. "At least, those of you who are not clocks never seemed to be so."

"We are too impossible to be anything but clockwork," the watch said. "All of us. Impossible."

The message that was written in the little damask-velvet book, which Alice never read, was this:

Once upon a time, there was a little girl who was horrible and wonderful at the same time, who was the heart of my heart; within arm's reach, yet so far away as to be unable to be reached at all.

At first I was allowed to be delighted and terrified by turns, but then I was banished from her side, through no fault of my own.

—Or was there fault?

For I taught her to think what she should not think, and did not teach her how not to say what she should not say, for I thought her perfectly enchanting the way she was.

But, alas, the world is what it is, which is much like the world as it was, and that which is best in life could not endure forever, and little girls who are enchanting may grow up to be young ladies who are less so, and whose Imagination are left to stifle and smother, and turn sour and wondering: what if, what if?

I can never answer the question for you, Alice, of what might have happened, or even what did *happen.*

That which occurs happens to us individually. With the smallest change in perspective comes what seems to be the greatest of transformations. One has only to turn 'round on a familiar road in the dark to understand this—the everyday has become the dangerously strange.

What you see here, Alice, is only an old man's imagination. Who the woman will be who sees it, whether she be young or old, grieved or joyful, I cannot say—but still I think I know her a little, for I knew her dreams once or twice, and that is no small thing.

I have always loved you, since the first time I saw you, but it was a love that changed according to the seasons, and never was as passionate as yours was for the young man whose promises had to be released into the sky, like awkward butterflies, to be gobbled up by egrets, sharp of beak and steely of eye. My affection for you has only been fond, and playful, and by turns regretful, for I have caused you such Trouble.

I wish that we had written more letters to each other, afterward, but then again I would be dreadfully sorry to be found out as such a bore! For it is easy to enchant a child, harder to enchant a young woman (as you know, I have never been able to master such a thing), and harder still to enchant (or even to entertain) the mother of small children. I am over-particular; if you had had girls instead of boys, I might have tried.

By the ticking of the clock, it is well past midnight, and if I am to dream my dreams, I must begin soon—for dawn shall arrive, and then I shall awake, and the dream will burst like a bubble, and I will never know how it begins, let alone ends, if I do not cease writing this note to you.

I shall take my dose of—well, perhaps it's better that you don't know what it is; I know how curious you are. It would be best if you never tried it yourself; it makes one feel so strange, and to see inside another's dreams is not a gentle thing.

When I wake, I shall whisper what I have heard to the painter who I have hired to paint your wedding-gift, and hope that the painting will open a way into your dreams, so that you can see them, once again, for yourself.

Here I am rambling again, and the minutes pass stealthfully by. I shall take my dose, here, and then sign my last letter to you—

Yours, Charles.

P.S. As I wait for the dose to take hold of me, I shall write you a few notes on the rules of Wonderland. First, the Directions are as follows…

The White Rabbit leapt through the hole between the gears—there was a dreadful slicing sound—and then he spun through the air at a dizzying angle—rolled—and tried to stand, but could put neither hand nor foot underneath him to steady himself. He was sick with disorientation as he rocked back and forth on the brass floor of the landing outside the prison cell.

He once again tried to push himself up and heard the scrabbling of his paws on the metal, but it seemed to have no effect.

Ah. He was upside down.

He patted himself with his paws: fur in place, seemingly undamaged. He patted the place where his watch would have been, remembered that not only had the watch been confiscated, but that he wasn't wearing his waistcoat, and then felt the horrible scrape of the gears below him as they turned.

He shuddered and looked to the side: had he not made it through the walls of the cell after all?

No. He was safe.

Then the fur on his back pinched, then was caught between the gears and began to pull away from his flesh. He shrieked in horror and pain, the terrible sound of a Rabbit who has lost the gravitas of silence.

The gears still had him.

He turned his head to look toward the cell.

It could not be—and yet it was.

His body lay on the other side of the moving gears, white fur and all, not the slightest hint of blood, only the glimmer of brass. It rolled to the side, arms and legs moving desperately as they tried to escape the crushing gears.

In a daze of horror, the White Rabbit watched as his body suddenly bent in half and made a grinding sound, one of metal rather than bones or flesh. The gears of the cell tried to turn, but could not; they were jammed.

His arms and legs waved feebly.

The head of the White Rabbit—for that was all that he was—moaned softly to himself: "Oh dear…whatever shall I do without the rest of me…?"

The gears of the cell shuddered, and a horrible wrenching sound echoed through the tower. The White Rabbit's body slumped forward and went limp.

The terrible pain of his body being crushed by the gears ceased abruptly, and the legs flopped loose on the floor, and the torso slid into the gap between gears, and was gone. He heard the sound of it falling down what must have been a long chute, echoing and banging all the way down.

One leg toppled in after it; the other began to spin in a slow circle. Soon it, too, would be gone.

Well.

The Red Queen's sentence, which she had delivered against him so uselessly, yet so often, had finally caught up with him at last—in reverse. Now he was nothing *but* a head, and he must find some way yet to save Wonderland. The urgency had increased even as his ability had drastically decreased.

Rocking his head back and forth, the White Rabbit was able slowly to turn in the direction of the door to the small landing where his cell had rested, at the top of the tower: the doorway was barred, so that one might stand on the stairs and look inside to the cell itself.

The Great Chronometer never ceased from its continuous din; the city ticked and tocked and whirred and rang with every moment. And yet it was possible to hear such sounds as were not regular after a time, and the White Rabbit had spent enough time in both the daylight and moonlight Wonderlands that he had very good ears (fortunately still attached) indeed.

What those ears heard was that someone was climbing the stairs of the tower, and approaching all the nearer as it climbed.

Something must be done; and, as there was no one else, it was left to the White Rabbit to do it.

He had not investigated the landing outside his cell previously, having focused all his attention upon exiting the cell first. Once he had escaped, he reasoned, he would be able to proceed from there.

Now he regretted that decision. If only he had known that it would be "off with his head!" and leave him more or less helpless on the floor, waiting for a guard to discover him! His efforts to escape had been worse than useless.

He nevertheless examined his circumstances as closely as he was able.

While he did so, he muttered to himself, as was his wont:

"Landing…brass plate for the floor…bars over the doorway to the single set of stairs…walls made of fitted plates of copper…window at the far side of the tower…overlooking what I haven't the slightest…sky still starry and dark, brightly lit by moonlight…no apparent way out…"

By rocking his head back and forth and using his ears to push, he was able to roll himself across the floor toward the barred doorway, even as the footsteps increased in volume.

His plan was this: he would hide alongside the doorway of the tower, out of sight from the door. When the door had opened and the guard had entered, he would quickly roll through the doorway and down the spiral staircase that led down the tower.

He would roll more and more quickly as he fell, and thus be able to evade the guard.

What he was supposed to do when he came to a stop, he hadn't the slightest idea. He had no doubt that, whatever befell him, he would look back upon it and wish that he had taken more time to plan, looked further ahead (ha-ha), and been more patient.

The head that looked ahead and the head that looked back were both equally unfair, he realized, thinking only of themselves and not of circumstances which they did not currently face.

The steps grew louder and louder, until he could see the light in the stairwell shift with the guard's shadows. The stairwell was made of the same brass as the walls, in overlapping, bolted plates. The stairs were grillwork, and showed dim light through the rough treads.

Ting…ting…ting…

The top of a head appeared at the furthest stair. It wore a kind of flat metal cap, a soldier's cap, made of brass. Underneath it was a small head, enameled bright yellow, with two stubby horns on either side of the cap. Its eyes were beady and black, and it had a brass snout that turned up at the end, as if the creature was in a permanent state of having just smelled something particularly repugnant, so repugnant that its nose had begun to turn upwards to avoid it. The rest of the body that followed was that of one of the winding-beetles, armor enameled in bright green.

The Beetle paused at the gate and leaned forward, all the better to get a look into the White Rabbit's former cell.

Outside the cell, the White Rabbit suddenly noticed, were a few fragments of fur, that had spread themselves about in the light breeze coming from the window. He could hear the clink and clank of his remaining leg turning 'round and 'round inside the cell. He held his breath for a moment, then remember that he didn't actually need to breathe, and stopped. But still he *hoped*.

The winding-beetle grunted and clicked its upturned mandibles together, then turned about and began walking down the stairs, without ever having opened the bars covering the door to the stairs.

"Late!" the White Rabbit snarled to himself, as softly as he was able. It was the worst curse that he knew. "Late, late, *late*."

The Beetle hesitated on the stairs for a moment; the White Rabbit could see the back of its head, and the shuddering of its horns.

Then it continued down the stairs, leaving him to his fate.

Alice stamped her foot: "Oh! If only I had not lost the Watch. It could tell me where to go."

For she had tried every way she could think of to escape the little clearing in the frozen Winter garden, but as yet had not been able to leave it.

"I'm sure it could," said the Reverend Dodgson.

She gave him a suspicious look; he had almost used an ironic tone of voice. "You're sure it knew where to go, or you're sure that it could tell me to do so? It was the White Rabbit's Watch; I should think that at least it should know how to begin."

"*Was* it the White Rabbit's watch?" Reverend Dodgson asked. "How did you know?"

"It said so, and I have no reason to doubt it."

"Which means that therefore it must be true?" Reverend Dodgson asked.

She stamped her foot again. "That's not it at all! One cannot spend one's time questioning everything and everyone. One must…learn to see the best in everyone! At least until it is proven otherwise! Or else one would do nothing but ask questions all day, and never have any answers!"

She was almost ready to cry. At one moment Reverend Dodgson would be clever and enchanting, and the next he would set her on a line of inquiry that would end in nothing but tragedy. "Too many questions!" her mother had said of him once, before she had had him banished from the house.

"Must one?" Reverend Dodgson said relentlessly. "Or ought one to ask discreet questions, to discover whether the people surrounding one are trustworthy or otherwise?'

"I haven't the slightest idea."

Reverend Dodgson took her hand in his; it was cool to the touch, and suddenly she wondered whether he, too, were an automaton, such as her mother had proved—or merely cold. He began to lead her about the icy fountain in the center of the clearing again.

"What question might you ask of me, to find out whether I am who I seem to be?"

Alice took a deep breath: she hadn't been able to find her way out of the clearing on her own; perhaps Reverend Dodgson's elocutions would prove useful if she attended to them faithfully.

"One could take a direct approach and ask you whether you are who you seem to be. Are you Reverend Dodgson?"

"What a question!" Reverend Dodgson exclaimed, then winked at her.

"I could…" she considered the next line of attack. He *had* said that Wonderland was an indirect sort of place. "… One could see if one could make the person being questioned answer in a way that showed a discrepancy from their ordinary behavior."

"Such as?"

"Oh, any question would do. How are you? How do you like the weather?"

"I am well, thank you, and I like the weather well enough." He held out a hand. "It is, as you can tell if you examine my hand closely, neither raining, nor snowing, nor showering us with cake."

She nodded. It was the kind of thing he *would* say: but that was not proof.

"It is almost as though a polite conversation were a way of playing a game of identity, and cleverly hiding whether one were oneself or someone else," she muttered to herself.

Reverend Dodgson did not reply; he often did not, when she was thinking the type of thoughts he wished her to think.

"Another possibility would be to refer to memories that only the true person would know," Alice said. "Such as mentioning the time that you took our photographs dressed as Esquimaux, and Mother the explorer John Ross."

Reverend Dodgson's delicate eyebrows stretched to their furthest extent, giving him a comically froglike expression. "And that would be a clever enough trap among many members of society," he said, "unless they knew that they were being tested, and then might not they say, 'I don't have the slightest memory of such a thing'?"

"They might," she admitted. The trap had been reversed upon her again; while Reverend Dodgson had never taken such pictures, she should not have inserted her mother into the lie, for anyone with the slightest understanding of her mother would know that she would not have put up with such nonsense.

They circled the fountain again with no end in sight.

"And, further," said Reverend Dodgson, "What if such a test would be easy enough to foil as a Wonderlandian? One might *believe* oneself to be a perfectly ordinary person, with all one's memories seeming to be in place, and yet still be only a kind of copy."

"A mechanical tracing machine, a…a…" said Alice. She couldn't quite remember the word that she wanted.

"A pantograph," Reverend Dodgson said. "One might make the copy appear bigger, or smaller, or upside-down—one might make coins or statues or even clockwork, using such a machine."

"But could one make clockwork out of a person?" she asked.

"Certainly one could copy the exteriors of form."

"How would one copy a memory? Or a personality?"

"Hmmm," said Reverend Dodgson. His free hand stroked his chin. "I had only got as far as supposing that if one took enough photographs, one might be able to copy the person's expressions—a smile, a frown; vincerejection; horripilation."

Alice laughed. "Vincerejection? Horripilation? What are those things?"

"Vincerejection is the feeling one has when one suddenly understands that in order not to lose, one must therefore not win; or else when one realizes that in order to win, one must take an action so outside one's wishes that one would rather lose."

"That sounds terrible," Alice said.

"In either case, it is a sensation both unpleasant and no-ble," Reverend Dodgson agreed.

A cry came out of the maze surrounding the clearing; it raised the hairs on Alice's arms and all along the back of her neck. "What was that?"

The cry came again, desperate and keening.

"Oh, that is the cry of the Jubjub bird," Reverend Dodgson said.

It certainly sounded desperate enough, but if that were the case, then Alice should have remembered the sound—it sounded as though some poor soul were being murdered.

The cry came again, louder than before, and echoed all about the garden.

"Oh!" Alice cried, letting go of Reverend Dodgson's hand and putting her hands over her ears. "What a terrible sound!"

Reverend Dodgson tried to reply just as the bird cried again, and she was unable to hear him.

Just then, she caught sight of someone trying to burst through the hedge surrounding their clearing: the cry grew louder, and Alice could make out words through her hands over her ears: "Help, help!"

She sprang toward the hedge, uncovering her ears.

"Here, here!" she cried, reaching out her hands.

"Alice—!" shouted the Reverend Dodgson. "Don't—!"

But it was too late.

Alice plunged her hands into the hedge and grasped the hands that were trying to come through to her. The hands clasped her own and pulled her through.

The Red Queen walked, holding on to the bar in front of her, fuming at the brass plate which had been fastened over her mouth, so that she could not speak.

Normally, she maintained that her only problem with the system under which she labored was that *she* should not have to labor under it.

But today—now that it seemed as though the girl, Alice, might be able to help them, by upsetting the Golden Court, if nothing else—she could admit that if it was beneath her to labor so (and she could), then she could also admit that it was a labor beneath the dignity of all of Wonderland.

The metal mesh underfoot creaked as it turned on its axle. The enormously complex city of machinery that was the Great Chronometer stretched far overhead. Every platform, every wall, every alley was populated by day-lit Wonderlandians. They glimmered and sparkled in the moonlight, for every shred of dignity had been taken from them, and now they appeared without their clothes, or flesh, or fur, only naked clockwork that seemed to meld with the gears upon which they worked.

Their jaws, too, had all been locked closed, so that they could not even speak to one another, to pass the dull hours in tale or song or gossip.

Some of them, like her, trod upon turning bands of metal mesh; others had to turn winding-keys and winding-crowns; still others had to climb mechanical stairs that took them no further upward at the end of the night that they were at the beginning; some had to lift heavy bars; others to turn wheels or pull ropes. There was no hesitation, no break for food or water or rest, only the work—the work—the dull, plodding work.

The Red Queen made a point never to meet the eyes of another Wonderlandian; perforce she must look some-where, and thus could not prevent herself from seeing another wretched bit of machinery, forced once again to remember that from whence it had come, but at least she could pretend that she hadn't.

At the end of every night, just before dawn, all work would cease, and the Wonderlandians would find the wind-ing-gear nearest to them, and place the heel of their left foot, or the palm of their right hand, or the back of their head to the winding-gear—they had all been built with a socket for it. The Red Queen's socket was on the top of her head, so that she was forced to upend herself in order to be wound. A *most* undignified position.

Once the Wonderlandians were in place, the winding-gear would turn and wind them. It happened quickly, so quickly that it felt as though a hundred bees had been let loose in one's skull, and one became so dizzy for a time that one was unable to think or act or even shout for a few moments.

She had only partially listened to what the White Rabbit had been trying to tell her, before he had been arrested, but it seemed to have stuck in her mind, so that she was forced to think about it as she walked.

The daylit Wonderlandians were not actually winding the Mainspring.

It was a thought not to be considered—and yet she was so bored that she considered it.

It confused her. It was something having to do with the notion that a Wonderlandian ticked all day and all night, but only worked at night—one *half* of the winding that it used every day.

But then the White Rabbit had said something about the sun and the moon and the Central Palace and all the moonlit Wonderlandians, which became mindless gears in the Master Chronometer, but did not work: who was winding *them?*

The Red Queen's work throughout the night was strenuous and dull, but it was not something that could make the whole world turn 'round, no matter how many gears were used to increase it—Wonderland moved slow, but not *that* slow.

It was almost possible to believe that the extra winding came from the Mainspring itself. It was so big and so impressive a spring that it seemed as though it should last forever, no matter how much winding or unwinding was done by the creatures of Wonderland.

Alas, that was not the case. The Mainspring *was* unwinding.

The Red Queen did not believe in impossible things; that was the White Queen's province, whenever that silly woman bothered to be organized enough to not putter about as a Sheep.

It being impossible to believe impossible things, the Red Queen was forced to consider the alternative: the daylit Wonderlandians were being treated as slaves for some useless and trivial purpose, and that someone, somewhere, had lied to her about the reason for it.

She would find that liar, and remove its head.

A pair of winding-beetles walked slowly down her alley of the Great Chronometer, making sure that all was well, and that none of the daylight Wonderlandians had stepped free of their place, or had broken, or any other disorderly thing.

Their brass caps, stubbed horns, brass boxes full of care-fully-ordered tools, and green armor marked them as me-chanically inclined and less likely to meet out punishment to a Wonderlandian out of place: they only cared that the Great Chronometer was in order.

They did not acknowledge her as they passed, not even the slightest nod.

It set her gears on edge but was perfectly routine: if one was not broken, it was as though one did not exist.

Behind them followed another winding-beetle in brass cap and with its box of tools: it was traveling singly, and that was unusual of itself. Also of note was the fact that it locked eyes with her for a moment, as if trying to ensure that it had her attention.

She stared over its shoulder, waiting to see what it would do.

It approached her slowly, following the same path as the previous two winding-beetles.

Closer and closer it came, until it was beside her: sud-denly, it looked down, and almost as though drawn by a magnet, her eyes followed: in a slim claw it held a gear, an ordinary gear marked with a loose spiral in a cloudy, jewel-like tint: cherry juice.

When it was sure that she had seen the gear, its claw turned the gear on edge and slipped it into its toolbox.

She followed the third winding-beetle with her eyes until she would have been forced to turn her head; then she looked away.

A sign. She had been shown a secret sign—or rather a discreet sign—of something that previously she had only known through rumor brought to her by the White Rabbit: *the Great Unwinding*.

Previously, seeing it would have caused her frustration and despair.

Now, she was heartened.

The Mad Hatter's Watch explained to Alice Hargreaves its workings: that north was six, south was three, west was twelve, and all the rest should be obvious; and that now that they were in the Garden, the correct direction was no longer six but three, or south, or what-might-have-been, or Spring. When she inquired whether he meant "spring" as the season or "spring" as a part of a watch, the Watch clapped its mouth shut so hard it caused its hands to twitch.

It was almost as though the Watch were trying to confuse her for some reason. It was, no doubt, lying, at least in some regard.

When she tried to ask it further questions about the Great Unwinding, it only told her to "hurry, hurry," as though she were some sort of child to be so easily distracted.

"Sha'n't," she said. She had been walking around the fountain in circles; as soon as the Watch began to press at her to follow its direction (it wanted her to do a little shuffled dance-step to the right), she sat on the ledge of the fountain again and began to lean toward the water, and the turning statue of the woman pouring tea.

The Watch shuddered again.

"Tell me more about the Great Unwinding," she commanded it. "Having a need to replace or rewind a mainspring in a watch, *that* I can understand, but that has nothing to do with such a phrase: *the Great Unwinding*. It almost sounds as though you had the intention of destroying the mainspring, rather than replacing it."

She paused, waiting for the Watch to rebut her, but it stayed silent in her hand.

"But why would a *watch* want such a thing? Wouldn't a watch wish always to stay wound? And wouldn't it wish for its Mainspring to be kept safe for-ever?"

The Watch had grown slightly warmer in her hand, and had also begun to tick more loudly. The eyes within the sunlit clouds on its face stared at her coldly.

"Oh!" Alice exclaimed, as though she had only just thought of the idea. "*I* know. It's because once the Great Unwinding comes, only the wicked will stay unwound!

Those who have ticked and tocked in righteousness shall be saved. Isn't that how this sort of thing generally works?"

It was the sort of thing that Alice's mother had been in the habit of proclaiming; only a few of the words needed to be changed, to make it about the British Empire as well as something the Roman Pope might say, as easily as something out of the mouth of an adherent of the Church of England.

"The Great Unwinding," continued Alice, deprecatingly: she was trying to provoke the Watch. "Like a child who breaks his toys on purpose, because they are not quite to his liking." One of her sons, Carryl, had done that a few days before; she had refused his piteous requests to replace them—at least for the moment. "You shall have quite a shock, when they do not repair themselves to perfection."

The spout of the marble tea pot was approaching again.

The Watch kept its eyes on her, taking not the slightest glance toward the approaching stream of water this time. In a low, angry voice, it said, "Blasphemer!"

Then it began to ring loudly, a muddied, flat sounding ring that came from within its depths.

"*You* have never been filled up with butter!" it snarled, each word growing louder as it spoke. "*You* have never been dunked in tea—!"

It was just as ridiculous a thing as one of her sons might say, upon discovering that he would be made to perform some minuscule task which was immediately declared to be "unfair!"

A crashing sound began to echo throughout the garden in the distance, as though something were responding to the Watch's alarum.

"Shall I ruin you further, then?" she asked. "Shall I… dunk you?"

"*You* have never been packed solid with cherry-mash!" the Watch shrieked. "*You* have never had to tolerate a single offense in your life!"

Alice couldn't resist giving an evil chuckle, it reminded her of her boys so!

It struck her that it was an odd creation that Reverend Dodgson had left for her, an odd creation indeed, that rebelled against its creator so harshly that it wished everything smashed and rebuilt from nothing all over again!

"I know your maker," she said. "He was never a sensible man, but his creations were never so terrible as to deserve destruction. I forgave him of them long ago."

"MY MAKER!" shouted the Watch. "What do you know of *him*, that monster! When we are Unwound, we shall make of ourselves whatever we will!"

It had quite lost its temper; she almost felt a moment's pity for it.

"With what hands?" she asked it softly. "For yours shall be all unwound, and your maker is dead. The only one who might repair and wind you is me—and I have no skill at such things."

It had put itself into such a temper that it did not hear her, which was just as well.

A figure burst through the hedge and into the clearing; at the same moment, the Watch gave a lurch in her hands and leapt into the water of the fountain. She tried to grab for it, and missed.

As it sank—sinking a far longer distance than should have been possible in that shallow fountain—it seemed to grin at her as bubbles worked their way out from underneath its glass face.

Suddenly she was pulled up into the air. She gave a cry of surprise, and tried to twist 'round to see what had caught her: it was a metal beetle, covered in rust and soot, so dirty that it almost seemed furred.

It clicked as it picked her up in one claw.

She screamed again and thrashed her legs to try to kick her way free. The rusty beetle had taken hold of her nightdress, and with a tearing noise, the back of it tore free, and she dropped to the ground.

"Help! Help!" she shouted and ran directly away from the monster.

Unfortunately, her escape route led her straight into the hedge, where there was no escape.

She plunged into the twigs and leaves, not so much trying to escape as to burrow her way in deep enough that the beetle, with its sharp claws, would be unable to grasp her through the tangle of wood.

The hedge gave a little here and there, sliding around her, but on the whole kept her from moving.

"Help! Help!"

"Here, here!" Someone from the other side of the hedge was shouting at her.

Alice reached out with both hands. "Help!"

The monster's claw ran along her back, scratching her before the twigs turned the blow. The wound burned and stung.

Someone grasped her hands and pulled on her—*hard*—so hard that Alice felt dizzy, as if she were being turned on a wheel, fast enough to make the hedge in front of her blur—

PART III – THREE O'CLOCK –

WEST – AUTUMN – SMALLER –

WHAT-MIGHT-HAVE-BEEN

The White Rabbit hadn't the slightest idea what to do next: the bars between his head and the stairs were spaced too narrowly for him to fit through, no matter how he twisted and turned. He knew that he should have considered himself lucky that the removal of his head had not resulted in his immediate unwinding; however, he could not help but count himself a very poor Rabbit indeed.

A head! He was nothing but a head!

And soon he would become entirely unwound, for there was no winding-gear inside the cell. All he could do was to stay here, and wait, and hope to be rescued.

After an hour of such activity, he decided that the stories must have been mistaken: for there never was a Princess, let alone a Rabbit, who could make a career of waiting at the top of a tower for someone else to come and rescue them.

Ah, but what might have been, if only the guard had opened the door. If only…

Alice tumbled to the ground with her dress and pinafore puffing in a circle around her on the sun-warmed grass. Wherever she had gone, it was no longer Winter. The figure who had been crying for help had pulled her entirely through the hedge; now she was on the other side of it with her head spinning and her stomach all a-tumble.

A large, dark shape reached for her; out of well-honed instinct formed from avoiding her sister, Alice rolled to the side.

A sinister screeching noise came from the ground where she had been a moment ago.

Alice clambered to her feet and stumbled dizzily away from the darkened shape, to the other side of a white fountain that seemed identical to the one she had just left.

She ducked down behind one of the mermaids and rubbed at her eyes, hoping to clear them. After mashing her eyes with her fists several times, she peered over her shoulder to get a look at the large figure that had been trying to catch her.

It had not given up, and in fact was about to catch her again: an enormous, rusting metal roach, larger than a man and with pointy, sharp claws at the ends of its legs. It was directly in front of her.

Alice pushed upward and backward as hard as she could, and fell into the fortunately unfrozen mermaid-fountain with an enormous splash. The roach swung at her twice, with each of its two largest claws.

She dove under the surface for safety.

Something shiny lay at the bottom of the pond. Alice kicked hard, diving deeper after it.

It was the Watch!

She grasped it with one hand and tugged it upward with her. It was still large and heavy and ungainly, but it seemed to be trying to help her, opening and closing its cover in order to propel itself upward, like some sort of odd clam.

As they rose, Alice swam for the opposite side of the fountain, hoping to avoid the rusted roach, but when her head broke the water, she saw that she had come no closer to the edge at all.

In *any* direction. The tiny fountain seemed to have become quite enormous.

She lifted the Watch out of the water and balanced it upon her head, but it would not stay there: and so she rolled onto her back and placed the Watch onto her stomach. She kicked off her shoes and proceeded to float in the warm water of the pool, giving a little kick now and then in order to paddle herself eventually to the other side. In the meanwhile, she looked for the roach, for now she could not see where it had gone, or even where the statue at the center of the pool was. The mermaids had disappeared as well.

When she was sure that the Watch was not about to slide off, she murmured softly, "Are you all right?" She could feel it ticking ever so weakly.

The Watch gave a snort, then began to leak water from 'round its watch-stem. Its cover opened fully, catching the moonlight.

"Oh, woe," said the Watch. "I was thrown into the pool, and now I am damaged."

"Damaged?"

"I am *quite* waterlogged. Fortunately…" It trailed off.

"Fortunately what?"

"Fortunately I am a hardy watch."

"I'm glad," she said. "Have you seen Reverend Dodgson? Has he been here?"

"How would I know?" asked the Watch. "*I've* been under water this entire time."

"Who would do such a thing to you?" Alice asked.

The Watch harrumphed and would not answer.

Alice twisted and writhed, checking to see if she had come any closer to the edge of the fountain: she had not. In fact she seemed further away than ever. The edge of the fountain seemed a distant shore, one that she might never reach, especially if she were caught in a current.

"Oh, dear," she said. "I only hope you are not *too* broken to tell me which way to go. Otherwise we shall be swept out to sea."

"To sea?" asked the Watch. "Lift me up. I cannot see."

The Watch was too heavy to lift off her stomach without tipping herself into the waves, but Alice was able to tilt it to one side and then the other, so its face could look about.

"Hmmm," said the Watch. "We seem to be going in the wrong direction."

"No matter which way I turn—" Alice began to say.

"You've turned smaller," said the Watch. "And now you must turn larger again."

"Is that what it is to be larger or smaller?" asked Alice. "A direction? I've always wondered."

"*Some* people call it a direction," the Watch said. "*I* call it a dimensional nuisance, and I've known some dimensional nuisances!"

"Oh?" asked Alice.

The Watch, still tilted on her stomach, seemed to give her a sidelong look. "Never mind," it said. "Look, we've got to stop getting smaller and head in the opposite direction, but not too quickly—it wouldn't do for you to obliterate Wonderland with one careless kick!"

Alice agreed that this would be a *very* bad idea, although she wasn't the least bit sure how it could come about, other than if someone had labeled the entirety of Wonderland with a note saying *EAT ME!*

The Watch had her turn it this way, then that—until finally it gave out a pitiable sigh and said, "It's no use, Alice. I'm damaged, and my hands won't turn the direction that they ought to be turning."

"What direction is that?"

"Three o'clock—what might have been, that is. Ah, if only we could have turned toward what might have been. *Then* we would have all sorts of possibilities. For example, we might have been rescued by a passing boat, or ridden off on a beggar's wishes, or married someone else entirely!"

Alice laughed. "But I haven't married anyone *yet*," she said. "How can I have married someone *else*?"

The Watch ignored her. "I, for example, might have never been broken, or my cousin—"

Its words broke off; once again Alice had the sensation that the Watch had been about to say something that it did not wish her to hear.

"Or you might have belonged to someone else entirely," Alice said. "Instead of having been the White Rabbit's Watch, you might have been—oh, you might have belonged to the March Hare! And then where would you be? Stuck forever at six o'clock."

She had just noticed that the hands of the Watch were stuck in such a position, which was what had made her think of it just then.

"WHAT IS THAT YOU SAY?" the Watch asked in a terrible

voice. "I SHOULD NEVER HAVE BELONGED TO THE MARCH HARE! NEVER! "

It began to shudder all over, so that Alice threw an arm over it, lest it shiver its way back into the fountain and be lost forever—there was no way, with as large as the fountain was, that she could dive down after it *now*.

"THE MARCH HARE IS A MONSTER! AN ABUSER OF WATCHES, JUST AS HIS FRIEND THE MAD HATTER HAS BEEN KNOWN TO MURDER TIME! I CAN BEAR IT NO LONGER! THIS IS NO ALLIANCE, IT IS A TRAVESTY!"

The Watch was opening and closing its cover so violently that she did not know whether she would be able to hang on much longer.

"Stop, stop!" she cried. "You'll tip yourself over in a moment if you keep on like this!"

"I'LL MURDER HIM! I'LL PRY HIS COVER OFF AND STUFF *HIS* WORKS WITH BUTTER!"

Alice began to have the suspicion that the Watch had not entirely told her the truth: for it seemed to be *quite* wroth with the March Hare, and the Mad Hatter besides, and why would the watch which had never had anything to do with either of them feel such a way?

"THE RASCAL! THE RACLETTE! THE RAPSCALLION!"

The Watch continued in such a manner that Alice had to hold onto it with *both* hands, and soon began to sink from all the leaping about the watch did upon her stomach and chest.

No matter how she begged it to stop, the Watch would keep shrieking curses at the March Hare and the Mad Hatter. Finally it leapt upon her so hard that she was knocked quite into the water, so that she sank down underneath the surface from head to foot, and had to kick quite hard, lest she begin to sink in earnest.

The surface of the water had become choppy, as if whipped into peaks by a storm, even though the air was still and the sky clear, so that the stars twinkled peacefully overhead. The edge of the fountain had grown even further still, so that it was a fine line of white that ran along a distant horizon.

"I shall drown at this rate!" said Alice to herself. "But what about the Watch?"

She patted all over herself, but found no sign of it. She took a deep breath and dove under the waves, but saw no sign of it, not even the silvery shimmer of metal.

The Watch was gone.

She swam back up to the surface and trod water, trying to keep her head above the waves but finding it difficult; the peaks of every wave seemed determined to toss themselves on the top of her head.

"I must find—" The waves splashed over her head, and she spluttered, "I must find how to turn in the direction of what might have been!"

She swam in every direction; she even swam downward as far as she could, before she began to choke and was forced to swim upwards again. But it seemed to be impossible: she could not find the right direction, and the edge of the fountain had gone so far away from her that it had disappeared.

"What shall I do?" she cried, in between peaks of the waves. "Whatever shall I do?"

The waves had only grown bigger still. The waves pulled away from her, leaving her at what seemed to be the bottom of a great bowl, then began to rush at her all at once.

"Help, help!" shouted Alice, although she had few hopes of being rescued. "Help!"

The waves roared down at her. Any second, they would collapse upon her!

She swam harder—

The waves crashed down upon her and—

Alice dragged herself onto shore with both elbows, coughing up a great deal of water, that felt as voluminous as the fountain into which she had sunk. She looked up: she had arrived on the shore of a desert island, whose beach was as pure white as the marble of the fountain.

After a few dozen yards, the beach ended as suddenly as a sneeze, and there rose a jungle of green tangled trees and vines. The edges of the jungle were thick brush, and palm trees rose behind them. A tall palm tree rose above all the rest, twice as tall as any of the others. A small tan shelter made of palm-fronds and saplings rested on the sand just outside the greenery.

The air was still; Alice could hear a cacophony of birds shrieking back and forth. The air smelt of freshness, and not much of fish or seaweed. The branches of the tallest tree shuddered, and it seemed as though a dark shape peeped out at her from between the branches.

A woman in a long, dark dress and a white blouse—she looked like the statue of the woman in the fountain—stepped out of the jungle and waved at her. "Hallooo! Alice! Do come up to the shelter, it's so hot out on the sand!"

It *was* hot, and Alice was terribly thirsty, so she got to her feet, brushed out her dress (which was quite dry), and began to make her way up to the jungle. The shelter held two wicker chairs and a small bamboo table; the woman seated herself at one of the chairs and began fanning herself with an ivory-colored fan.

The closer that Alice came, the harder it became to walk. Her arms and legs seemed heavy, almost as though they made of stone.

Finally, Alice could come no further.

"Oh, I rather think that is far enough," announced the woman under the shelter. "If you walk any further, I shouldn't be the least bit surprised if something unpleasant happened to you, and you're heavy enough that I shouldn't be able to move you at all to rescue you."

Alice stopped, panting with exhaustion.

"I'm sorry to have made you walk all the way up the beach," the woman added, "But it *is* rather hot."

Alice frowned at this. "Whatever do you mean?" The words came out slowly and a little slurred, and deeper than her normal voice. She put a hand up to her mouth—the hand took several seconds to arrive.

"You and I," said the woman, "Have come to a place known as 'what might have been.' Have you heard of it?"

"Yes," Alice said slowly.

"I received a message some time ago, from someone who claimed to be from Wonderland, and who wished me to take the place of someone known as the Watchmaker. I decided to come a short way to see what it was all about, and whether I approved of such a thing. Do you understand?"

"Nooooo," said Alice.

"Then I sha'n't continue explaining it to you. But know this: I am another Alice, from another place, and the two of us are meeting at the very furthest edges of Wonderland, which is where you are from, and England, which is where I am from."

Alice wanted to explain that she, too, was from England, but thought that the effort would exhaust her, and clarify nothing to the other woman, who did *not* resemble her in the slightest. Alice didn't like her; she had *such* a willful, spoilt face.

"There are many Englands," the woman said. "And so I may not be the *only* grown-up Alice that you meet, especially on the far edges of things."

"Why?" Alice managed to squeeze out.

"Why? Why am I here? Why did I want to see you?"

Alice nodded.

"Well, for one thing you were making an utter mess of your adventures here. To be lost at sea in a fountain, really? Abandoned by your guide, and not much further than you were when you started off, and here it is, almost three-fifths of the way through the night! You haven't the slightest idea of how to save Wonderland, do you?"

Alice shook her head.

The woman opened her mouth to continue haranguing—then stopped and frowned at Alice. "For another thing—I wished to know." She raised one hand, palm out. "No, don't ask me what. I shall tell you in a moment."

She drummed her fingertips on the top of the table.

"I am…from an England where Mother was less ambitious. I have studied some of the worlds in which the Reverend Dodgson told the Wonderland story to us, to Ina and Edith and myself—to you and your sisters. It was a different story, of course. All the characters are different, even if some of the puzzles and jokes are the same. *Edith's Adventures in Wonderland*, it's called, after another Edith of his acquaintance—not your sister. The three of us were never important enough to have anything named after us. It is a book about a girl who goes on adventures after falling down the rabbit-hole—oh, I forgot—the White Rabbit is the same; he is the only character who is the same. He is late, just as Father was always late. All the others, quite different."

The woman made a face.

"I wished to know what it would be like, to have been *the* Edith—or rather the Alice. To have been famous, to have been immortalized, even if it only was as a child."

Alice opened one hand, then closed it again: she hadn't the slightest idea what the woman was talking about.

The woman abruptly stood up, sweeping her skirts around in a circle. She had a terrible look upon her face, as if she had just swallowed a bug. "I find that I make a very poor Edith, for I am not the least bit beautiful, or kind, or brave, or sensible, or sweet. I can see by your face that I am none of those things, and remain only the unworthiest of Alices. And so, call it pride if you will, I shall not come to wind you up again after your 'Great Unwinding,' or whatever it is called. Wind *yourselves*, if you can, for I sha'n't do it."

She whisked herself away into the jungle, leaving nothing but a few shaking leaves behind her.

"But—" Alice tried to call her back, but it was too late.

The woman's voice called: "Go home, Alice. Turn back while you still can, and take whatever pleasure you might in what Wonderland you have left. I assure you that the other one is far superior, even if it is named after someone else. This one is *rotten*."

Alice tried to reach out toward the woman—but it took

forever for her hand to stretch the length of her arm, and she lowered it again.

She did not know what else to do, so she turned back toward the ocean. With every step she felt better, lighter—more like an eight-year-old girl than a piece of stonework, a statue.

Wonderland *did* deserve to be saved, even if it *was* rotten.

Alice Hargreaves went flying through the air in her robe and nightdress, shrieking at the top of her lungs for fear of landing somewhere hard and breaking every bone in her body.

She did *not* land somewhere hard, but rather somewhere stiff and prickly: another hedge.

The branches stuck painfully into her back and she was flung forward, as if on a spring. She fell forward into the lawn, making her hands and wrists twinge painfully.

"*Ow*," she groaned, inhaling the sound like a pipe's smoke-ring.

She looked up: the automaton-beetle-soldier thing that had been pursuing her a moment ago was no longer in sight, although the clearing in which she found herself was otherwise much the same: except that it was winter. The leaves on the hedge had mainly fallen, the ice in the fountain was frozen, and the grass was chill with frost.

The sun had set and the moon had risen. Time had been stolen from her.

A deep breath, and she attempted to calm herself. She did *not* wish to find herself shrieking nonsense in the middle of an abandoned garden.

Then something moved on the other side of the fountain, and she realized that the garden wasn't abandoned at all.

Standing on the other side of the fountain was…

Was…

Reverend Dodgson.

He had aged, but not so much as he had before he had passed from England into whatever awaited him, be it heaven, hell, or something altogether stranger. His clothing seemed old-fashioned, which made sense—he seemed a man of fifty, at most. His brown hair was only slightly streaked with gray. His skin sagged, so that the corners of his mouth resembled those of a frog's. He wore a dark coat and waistcoat, and a watch-chain whose end hung loose: someone had taken his pocket-watch.

"Hello, Mrs. Hargreaves," he said.

She gasped breathlessly for a moment; she could not have said a word. The wind seemed to have been knocked out of her. Slowly, she pushed herself backward onto her knees and tried to catch her balance. The clearing still seemed to spin slightly—or else it was the sight of Reverend Dodgson unsettling her.

She finally caught her breath. "Hello, Reverend Dodgson."

He seemed unutterably sad. "You have come to put an end to all this, haven't you?"

"An end to all this?"

"To Wonderland."

She looked about herself: they were only trapped in a garden with no way out, or rather no *logical* way out. No entrances or exits: but always a way out, if only one could make sense of how to change direction.

"This isn't Wonderland," she said. "This is a…a neat little prison for catching Alices in."

He smiled, although his face was no less sad: "That may be more true than you know."

For a long, full moment, they stared at each other, or rather just past each other. Reverend Dodgson's eyes seemed fixed upon Alice's feet; hers looked upward, studying his face until the moment that she almost thought that he was about to look up at her, and then she looked away, studying the patterns in the moonlit, silvery clouds.

"Why?" she asked. "Why did you…"

She didn't know quite what to ask: had Reverend Dodgson built this place for her? Or had he discovered it?

"I'm dying," he said.

"I…" She didn't like to tell him that he already had.

"Wonderland is the sort of place that one only finds once or twice. I found it once, while telling you a story on our boating trip along the Isis; I found it again, when—the year you and your sister came to me for your last photographs. And then the years passed recklessly, as they will, and you were a young woman, and we cared very little for each other, and…"

"And you decided to use my marriage to Reginald as an excuse to try to come here again," she said. "The painting…it had very little to do with me, didn't it? It was simply the window you needed to return to Wonderland."

"That is true."

"If that *is* true, and I'm not admitting for one second that it is, then how was it that you remained in England afterwards?"

He paused, then coughed into his hand discreetly. "I may have…sent a mechanical man in my place. I might have described England so vividly, and so thoroughly displaying its nonsense, that he simply couldn't resist the opportunity to go."

He had returned his eyes to the safety of her feet; she took the opportunity to incredulously gape at his face.

"He lived until just a few years ago," Alice said. "And as far as I know, only your sister might have known what he was."

"I might have had concerns…that he would unwind quickly, and give the whole thing away. Was he…was he happy, do you think?"

Alice Hargreaves, the mother of three sons, blinked. "You sent a clockwork man here to die, and you wondered whether he was happy?"

"One *may* wonder, yes," he admitted, still staring at her feet.

"He was smug," Alice said. "A buttoned-up, prim, smug man who remained unstooped and oblivious to other people's feelings and concerns to the end, and became entirely without creativity, except that he published *Sylvie and Bruno* in…in 1895, or 1896, I can't remember which, which was the most triflingly dull satire on academia that could be imagined. I thought it was petty."

"Almost as if the life had gone out of him," Reverend Dodgson murmured.

"*Almost,*" Alice said. "*Almost* as if he had had little life within him to begin with."

There it was again, the old fighting between them. He *would* insist on being so heartless and cruel, though. More faithful in pursuit of his facts and ideas than in his friendships—but that was unfair, wasn't it? He had not left her; he had been driven off by her mother.

Nevertheless she couldn't see him as anything other than a fool, an unthinking fool, to send a clockwork man to England, in his place…

"I'm sorry," she sighed. "If ever I imagined that I would be able to speak to you again, this is not what I imagined or would have wanted it to be. Please forgive me."

She still felt stiff and judgmental, thoroughly unchristian: unimaginative.

"Of course I forgive you, Alice," he said. "When first I saw you, I said to myself…"

And then he said nothing.

She rolled her eyes, by necessity glancing upwards as she did so.

There were letters written in the clouds, made almost of finest lace rather than white puffs of ante-precipitation: *Now there is a cruel little girl, who will make the world as unhappy as she is, and it would be safer for us all if she were happier rather than otherwise.*

She forced her lips into a frown. It sounded like something one of her sons would say. Was it a thought passing across his mind, or something else? Surely it was not a coincidence.

"I don't know if I forgive *you*," she said. "You have always been incorrigible; once I started forgiving you I should have to keep it up for the rest of eternity, for you would never stop doing things that needed forgiveness."

"I haven't yet," he agreed.

"Oh, Reverend Dodgson," she said. "You really sent a clockwork man to take your place?"

He looked up at her, his blue-gray eyes, as always, giving her the sense of being weighed—not judged, but weighed, like the Egyptians who weighed their hearts against the feather of virtue.

"Perhaps he wished to go. Wonderland is not found to be pleasant by all, you remember. There were always children who found it rather terrifying."

Alice had never found it so—but she understood the sentiment. If only she had been a little less brave, or a little more sensible, she would have lost her wits.

But then, if she had been someone else—Wonderland should have been an entirely different story, and thus an entirely different place. In a way, all Wonderland's flaws were her own.

She sighed. "Reverend Dodgson, if I am ever to forgive myself for my own flaws, I must surely forgive you yours."

"So you sha'n't destroy Wonderland then?"

Her eyebrows rose. He was back to looking at her feet.

"I hadn't intended to destroy it in the first place," she said.

"Hadn't you?"

She shook her head. "I don't understand."

"Why did you come here, Alice?"

"I wished to find out—I was curious—"

She glanced upward: the white trail of thought was writing itself out as she watched this time. *I was angry that you should think that I needed this place in order to be happy, or to escape.*

"Charles," she growled, as if he were one of her sons. She was almost ready to spank him. "Get…out… of…my…dreams!"

The Red Queen trod on her metal mesh belt, one foot after the other, winding and clanking, winding and clanking. The monotony was unavoidable and torturous, as well as being a complete waste of time.

She *hated* being forced to think.

During the daylit hours, she had her heart's desires, each and every single one of them. She was waited on hand and foot, albeit incompetently, which allowed her to occasionally throw fits and behead anyone she chose: they were all asking for it, just by *breathing*. As well as through multiple other, more serious offenses, of course.

Every heart's desire but one, that was: that she not be forced to march all the night long as a slave.

Who would have done such a thing to her—to all of them?

The Red Queen, even now that the illusion of her flesh had been removed and she was little more than a brass skeleton marching along with tens or hundreds of thousands of others, shuddered.

Perhaps the situation had been caused by a kind of accident, so that it had happened once by chance, and now must happen in just the same way ever after, like a prince who, having been turned once into frog, must therefore continue as a frog, until the curse was somehow lifted.

It was an odd thought, but she considered it. Why not? She had the time. And in situations such as this, any sort of thought or emotion that might have some novelty to it was to be dwelt upon for as long as possible, or else one would be reduced to calculating times-tables inside one's skull, just to have a way to mark the passage of time.

Time: she could only just tell, between the solid towers of machinery around her, that the moon had slid past its zenith.

Some powerful creature wished to destroy Wonderland, or to enslave it—it couldn't be both, could it? No, it must be that one power enslaved them, and another wished them to be free.

—

"I am *not* about to destroy Wonderland," Alice Hargreaves said.

The lines around Reverend Dodgson's mouth deepened even further than before, making his plain yet arrogant froglike face even more ridiculous than before. He chewed on the inside of his cheek. "There are many Alices, and many Wonderlands," he said finally. "*One* of you is sure to do it, or at least to do nothing to save it."

"That explains nothing."

He continued to gnaw. "Some of the Alices never had Wonderlands."

She shook her head. "Charles, you are speaking madness. You must explain it to me, or I sha'n't be able to follow it, no matter how brilliant your reasoning might be."

He looked at her helplessly. "I don't know where to begin. I am a Christian, as you know."

"As am I," she said, although she suspected that her meaning of the term and his were not the same.

"I am a Christian," he repeated, "and thus believe that Creation was created by the Creator, and that Christ, his only begotten son, died for our sins, redeeming us."

Alice rolled her eyes and did a quick check of the clouds, but there were no hidden messages there.

"And yet," he continued, "I do not know whether *this* place belongs to the Creator, or can be considered to have been saved by his Son."

It must, trailed the clouds, but the letters were half-finished, only tentative. *As all things must…?*

"I have long wondered whether it was a place that came from my imagination, or was merely selected by it—had I been someone else, then perforce I must have found a different world and called it Wonderland. At least, that is what I wonder," Reverend Dodgson said. "And if it is not a place that I, myself, created—and thus being, by extension, the creation of the Creator—then is it outside His purview? Am I without hope of salvation? For I *am* dying, finally, and it concerns me that I may—"

"*Now* it concerns you?" Alice demanded. "*Now?*"

Reverend Dodgson closed his mouth with a snap, as if he had caught a fly.

"You are afraid that another Alice—whatever that means—is going to break Wonderland. You're afraid that you're outside of the purview of the Creator. You're dying. You've sent a clockwork man to its death, worlds away from home. You opened a way to Wonderland, not for a child, but for your own selfish reasons…and now that you're dying you wonder whether you might have made a *mistake*. Is that about right?"

He had gone back to studying her feet again.

"Wonderland can fall to pieces for all I care," Alice said coldly. "And so can you. I should be home…a mother to my sons, a wife to my husband, a pillar of my society, standing firm against chaos and disorder. Instead I am here. Oh, what a fool I am!"

She had come all the way to Wonderland: now she only wished to go home. Her innocence—that which had out-lived her ambitious mother and her rambunctious sons, at any rate—had been used up, the last dregs of moisture at the bottom of a dead well.

"My heart is broken, Charles," she said. "And you have broken it."

He seemed to have shrunk inside himself, as he stood on the other side of the fountain, so that his clothes no longer fit. Just before him, the statue of the prim lady in the center of the fountain stood frozen. The statue's eyes seemed to fix upon Alice's—almost accusingly.

She turned away—only to discover that an opening had formed in the hedges surrounding the fountain. She began to walk toward it; she had no further interest in whatever else Reverend Dodgson had to say, not about other Alices, not about other Wonderlands, not about Heaven itself.

"Alice—" said Reverend Dodgson, his voice fading, almost as though he were being carried distantly away. "Wait—!"

She didn't hesitate, but walked through the archway in the hedge.

And she didn't look back.

The green-armored winding beetle who had shown the Red Queen the sign of a spiral printed in cherry juice on the gear had returned, following the other oblivious winding beetles in their bronze caps, just as before. It still carried its toolbox.

As it passed, it showed her the spiral on the small gear again, and murmured in a low, mechanical voice, almost as though to itself:

"The Crown is the traitor. We join you, look for the sign. Attack before dawn."

How she wished her lips had not been sealed, and that she could ask the winding-beetle a question!

And then it was moving on along the row of anonymous, voiceless daylit Wonderlandians, murmuring to the next brass clockwork figure in line.

Dawn, was it? Allies, were they?

She had her doubts.

If the Crown were a traitor, then why had it been sending messages back and forth to her via the White Rabbit?

That the White Rabbit should be a traitor was ridiculous; he didn't have the gears for it. He was conscientious to his core, even if he was a coward. If ever he should decide to betray someone, he would warn them first, groveling as he did so.

And there was nothing in the messages that could be used against the Wonderlandians: they had discovered so very little.

However…

The White Rabbit had had complete access to *all* the secrets of her court. She had told him *everything*, even that which she did not choose to tell to the Golden Court. The

White Rabbit was the perfect sycophant: one could tell him anything, and he would agree with it!

But it wasn't the White Rabbit and if it wasn't the White Rabbit then who might have…?

Alice Hargreaves passed through the archway in the hedge. She kept her eyes fixed ahead of her as she followed the pathway through the hedge-maze, and began to walk quickly, then to run.

After a long time she stopped to catch her breath.

She looked behind her: the hedge had grown completely shut.

"Thank you…thank you," she breathed. She was shaking.

She had never thought Reverend Dodgson to be…any of the terrible things that rumors had said he was. She thought she had only hated him for abandoning her—a childish resentment over an event in which he truly was not at fault. And then she had despised him, as a young woman might, for letting her mother play her games with him, and force him to take photographs of her and her sister Ina, even when her mother would not speak to him socially.

He had always been taking pictures of them at her mother's behest. She had disliked her grasping, shallow mother—and so she had disliked anyone who would do her bidding, as she would a sycophant.

And then, as a grown woman, she had seethed with jealousy, for he was about it still: taking young girls and filling up their heads with nonsense.

Her nonsense.

But now she knew. After her marriage, it had no longer been *him*, but a poor clockwork man who had died alone and apart from his home and family. She had hated one who was better to have been pitied.

It had been unfair of her.

And now she could not find it in herself to hate Reverend Dodgson at all.

She *was* relieved that she no longer had to…to idolize him. He was no longer larger than life and twice as natural: she was ashamed of him.

Now that he could not see her—she tipped her head onto her hands—and wept—

Alice walked into the ocean, firmly turning her back on the jungle where she had met the other Alice.

She fumed: "Her head is one that I wouldn't mind having off. I'm not nonsense. *She's* nonsense." Her feet splashed in the water, which stayed quite shallow for a long time, the white sand of the beach stretching out under the water before suddenly turning green and dark. "I hope *her* Wonderland gets forgotten and a hundred years from now no-one will remember it all."

She muttered until the water reached her knees, then her arms, then her shoulders, and finally she was forced to swim, lest she have to walk along the bottom like a crab.

How she was to reach the Golden Court from here, she did

not know. Why had the Watch thrown itself about so? Surely it was at the bottom of the ocean by now, entirely filled with water, and being made into coral and nibbled at by fishes.

Ridiculous old Watch! How were they to save Wonderland now?

She paddled onward until the island of the Other Alice had almost disappeared into a thin white line. Before her was another low line of white beach. This one, however, shimmered with a golden luster over the white sand. She swam harder: was she approaching the Golden Court?

Something, at last, was beginning to grow a little larger.

The White Rabbit continued to wait, bodilessly, near the gate across the exit to his prison cell at the top of the tower in the Central Palace, twirling his ears slowly 'round each other and playing blinking games: first one eye, then the other. He had almost invented an alphabet when he heard the sound he was both dreading and lived in painful hopes of: footsteps on the stairs.

The footsteps seemed to take forever to approach him. Metal clanked against metal. The White Rabbit shoved his head as close as possible to the wall and prepared himself to make a quick roll for it.

He could see a little way into the staircase downward. He watched intently as the brass cap of a winding-beetle appeared, and then its head with its upturned snout, and then its green-enameled body, and then its toolbox…

It stopped on the stairs so suddenly that the White Rabbit almost exclaimed out loud, but he stopped himself in time, even without the benefit of hands to clap over his mouth.

The winding-beetle moved its claw, the one that was not currently holding the toolbox, to reveal that it held a loose gear. Upon the gear was the mark of a spiral, written in a red enamel or paint. The winding-beetle paused for a moment, then turned its claw so that the sign was hidden again.

"The Crown is the traitor. We join you, look for the sign. Attack before dawn."

Then it turned around and went back down the stairs.

The White Rabbit sighed.

Although he had never seen it before, only heard it described to him by the Hatter, he knew what the loose spiral must signify: it was the sign of the Great Unwinding. The conspirators must have mistaken him for an ally, now that he had been imprisoned.

They thought the Crown was the traitor, did they?

Traitors were one thing. Destroying the Mainspring was another.

If he had been trying to infiltrate the group, this would have been a rare bit of luck indeed.

But if he was to join an uprising against the Master Chronometer *now*, two things would first have to occur: the Red Queen would have to give him her permission, and *someone* would have to come and let him out of this prison and attach him to some feet.

—

Although it had been day-time when she had left the jungle island, the closer that Alice swam to the gold-topped island, the more it seemed that it was the moon above her, not the sun.

She reached the shore and climbed up onto the sand. Past the beach was what *must* be the Golden Court, or at least a brass one. An enormous brass plate ran to the edge of the sand and stretched as far as her eye could see. Just as the jungle island had been abruptly topped with green, this island soon became covered with gears and springs and escapements. In the distance it rose upward farther and farther until at last it became a great tower in the center.

"The Golden Court," Alice said, trying out the words to see if they fit. "I shall travel to that tall tower in the center, where there is sure to be someone who can help me save Wonderland."

She shook out her skirts (they were dry as soon as she had taken herself out of the water, although she did have a metal crab in her pocket that she had to dislodge and push back into the ocean), brushed her dark hair away from her face, and began to tramp across the loose sand underfoot.

Her limbs remained the same: not the least bit like stone.

The metal plate echoed with the sounds of clinks and clanks and whacks and whirrs and bells and whistles and, most of all, ticking. The sound began as something distant that competed with the sound of the waves on the shore, then grew louder and louder until it had drowned out the ocean entirely.

She was tempted to put her hands over her ears; then she almost ceased to notice the sounds entirely.

As she approached the plate, she saw that there were dozens of figures among the nearest gears—they were hard to see, because they were also made of clockwork. One of them saw her—it had been turning a low crank set onto the ground—and froze in place, as if startled.

It was all right; she would soon assure it that she had only come to help.

The figure began to move again, this time not turning the crank on the ground, but pulling itself against the crank as if it could not let it go. Its struggles became more and more frightening, the closer she approached; she almost thought it would tear off its arms.

But at last they came free, and the automaton came toward her, running as fast as it could.

Its large head, which stood on a surprisingly slender neck, began to shake back and forth with the utmost urgency: *No, no, no!*

"It's all right," she said. "I sha'n't hurt you. But I *must* go to the tall tower in the center of the Golden Court, don't you see? I must save Wonderland. I'm the only one who can do it, you know, for I am a girl, and cannot be stolen away and forced to work all night, the way you are. I don't know what it is that is causing this to happen to you, but I will find a way to stop it."

Tears came to her eyes; she had no way of knowing whether the figure in front of her was one of the Wonderlandians she had met—the Duchess, perhaps—or a complete stranger. Removing one's flesh was a terrible thing, and even worse, the automaton's mouth had been sealed over with a metal plate, so that all it could do was hum at her, waving its arms and shaking its head, just across the border of the enormous metal plate.

"Don't be so frightened," she said. "I promise that I won't hurt you."

No, no, no, the automaton continued to signal to her. *Don't, don't, don't.*

But Alice had never made it a habit to listen to what she was told to do, and so, as gently as she could, she turned the automaton aside, and stepped onto the plate.

The Red Queen looked up at a sound: there had been a subtle change to the cacophony of clanks and whirrs around her. She had become so used to the sound that she had forgotten how loud it was; now that she had been reminded of it, it had become overwhelmingly loud again, and drowned out the sound of whatever it was that she had just noticed.

Around her, nothing seemed to have changed. The innumerable daylit Wonderlandians worked at their useless, demeaning tasks, nothing more than machines—

But wait.

One of them was *not* working. The Wonderlandian was small, but not of the size of a bird, or a cat, or anything else which crept or flew or pounced in the woods. It was shaped like a person—a child, or a midget.

Had it been there a moment before, standing above the level of the Red Queen's head on a shallow ledge across the narrow alley?

She thought not.

And what was it doing? It struggled as if to free itself from the winding-machine to which it had been attached: a large, heavy wheel with multiple spokes, like the wheel of a sailing-ship, which had to be laboriously turned. The enormous wheel looked too massive for the small figure to move at all, let alone wind throughout the night.

The Wonderlandian had released its hands from the spokes—no difficulty there—and was now pulling with both hands at the chain that had been fastened to a hook on its waist, and the ledge underneath her.

After a few moments' struggling, the figure stamped its foot.

The Red Queen, despite having not the slightest illusion (at the moment) that she was of flesh rather than metal, shuddered and felt as though gooseflesh had appeared along her arms and the back of her neck. The figure continued to struggle with its chain while the wheel in front of it turned backwards, undoing whatever work she had done, before trying to escape.

A pair of winding-beetles turned down the alley and began trundling toward the new clockwork slave, in case it was broken.

The figure stamped its foot again: there was no mistaking it.

If the Red Queen had been able to speak she would have moaned. Her hopes had been shattered—and why shouldn't they? Hope was a kind of lie: for it certainly has nothing to do with what was actually happening before the Red Queen's eyes!

The figure before her, struggling with its chain and stamping its foot, completely unaware of the approach of the winding-beetles come to "repair" her, was none other than…

ALICE.

The moon had nearly set—but a few moments remained before it touched the far edge of the great city that was the Master Chronometer.

From the face of the moon, one might have seen a pair of winding-beetles climbing a pair of ladders in order to disabuse a small clockwork Wonderlandian of her notions of free will with a pair of heavy wrenches.

All must be disciplined, if only for half of the day; no matter how much freedom such souls were granted during the daylit hours, at night perforce they must work together, as a machine. Discipline above all: those who would not work deserved nothing.

Unfortunately, the two winding-beetles had not succeeded in returning the little Wonderlandian to her place; or, rather, they could force her to stay in one spot, they could even place her hands on the spokes of the wheel; but if they wished the wheel to turn, they had to do it themselves: the Wonderlandian, even as reminded as she was of her status—a machine among machines—could not be *made* to do the work.

And they could not make her foot to cease its stamping.

Near to her, other Wonderlandians were beginning to cease in their duties as they saw the clockwork girl struggle. They ceased their marching, their lifting, and their turning.

Other pairs of winding-beetles were sent from their places—they appeared out of panels hidden among the massive gears to try to stop the disturbance.

The winding-beetles began to restrain the daylit Wonderlandians who had managed to escape their winding-machines; other daylit Wonderlandians began to restrain the winding-beetles. Battles broke out. Machines were smashed. Chains were pried free, manacles were dropped between the teeth of moving gears, claws were beaten against plates, loose gears were seized for shields and beaten into armor.

The daylit Wonderlandian who had begun or rather inspired the struggle cowered on the ledge. The two winding-beetles stood on their ladders with wrenches upraised.

They could not make her work; therefore, they had the right of breaking her up and using her for spare parts.

A half-circle of Wonderlandians edged in behind the ladders, weapons in hand.

Just as the first of the winding-beetles swung its bar, the other Wonderlandians struck, smashing the two ladders at the base.

The winding-beetles flew up into the air for a moment, and their swings missed the clockwork girl. Then they overbalanced and fell backward into the half-circle of daylit Wonderlandians behind them.

In seconds it was over: the winding-beetles had been pulled to pieces. Only a few small screws and bolts rolling lazily on the metal plate remained.

There could be no battle-cry; the Wonderlandians' mouths were still sealed shut. But one of the tallest of them, whose head was now enclosed in a helmet made out of a beetle's head, raised a claw-footed mace over his head, swung it in a great circle, and pointed it toward one of the panels between the gears, through which another winding-beetle, quite startled, was just emerging.

The daylit Wonderlandians quickly pulled the new beetle to pieces as well.

If he had been able, the tall Wonderlandian would have cried out, "To the Mainspring!"

In a strange silence that was really the deafening sound of metal clanking and whirring and buzzing and ringing, they marched to the entrance of that tunnel and others that the beetles had used, broke down the doors, and went in.

The end of Wonderland had begun.

PART IV – TWELVE O'CLOCK –

SOUTH – SPRING –

GREAT UNWINDING – NEVER

Alice Hargreaves dried her tears and stood up straight, brushing the leaves and dirt out of her nightdress and robe, then pulling her long, dark hair out of its braid, combing the twigs out of it with her fingers, then rebraiding it.

She sniffed hard several times, then gave up and wiped her nose on her sleeve—just as her boys would do, if they weren't watched by their nurse. She was regressing back to childhood! She was lucky that Reginald couldn't see her now; he would have a good chuckle at her appearance.

She smiled in fond memory of other touslings. Well.

It hadn't been her first choice for a marriage—and they had had some rows, no denying that—but they had three good boys they both loved, and they kept from hurting each other too badly most of the time, and if she couldn't have said that she *loved* him, not in the mad and reckless way that poets *loved* (and not in the way she had loved Leopold, either), then—it was still a good partnership. A good marriage.

She wished he was with her, now—but of course it was too late; he still slept in the bed she had left only a few moments ago. In England, only a moment had passed.

When all of this was over—she would be home soon.

She took one last brush at her eyes and faced the path forward through the labyrinth (the one behind her having grown closed). It was quite dark; the moon had sunk down past the tops of the hedges. The frost crunched underfoot.

"Halloo," she called. "Is anyone there?"

As she wandered the labyrinth, she took only turns to the right, bypassing all the lefts—it was a good way to solve all but the cleverest labyrinths—but did not find another clearing, and certainly not a way out.

She began to break off twigs and leave them in the entrances of the turns she picked, in case she was going 'round in circles after all, but she did not cross her path again.

After a time she stopped, stamped a foot, and looked upward at the sky, wiping tears from her eyes. There were no stars, not in Wonderland, although she thought she saw a shadow flitting overhead. She retrieved her temper, took a deep breath, and continued on.

She turned right…turned right again…turned 'round at a dead end…turned right…turned right…

Finally, ahead of her was another archway. But whether it led out of the labyrinth or into another clearing, she could not see, for it was quite dark. She stepped toward archway; a low white shape lay on the other side: another fountain?

The leaves shivered, as if they were about to grow closed, and deny her an exit—horrible things! But she maintained her pace. She could rush forward on the icy grass and push her way through if need be, but until then, she still had her pride.

"Off with its twigs!" she hissed at the hedge, and smiled a little, to herself, when it drew back slightly from her.

Of course her boys liked the parts of the two Alice books that had swords and knights and fighting: the two older ones she had privately named *Dee* and *Dum* for all their fighting, and the youngest—Carryl—was always trying to invent things, and heaving mighty sighs when they went wrong. More than once she had chased after them, pretending to be the Red Queen, or the Jabberwock, or some other creature of Wonderland from whom they should be forced to squeal and run.

The archway remained open. She stepped through, into another clearing—another challenge—another frustration—another useless confrontation in a plotless dream. She wanted to go *home*.

The hedge rustled behind her; she glanced back; it had grown closed.

But when she looked back into the clearing, a painfully bright light shone into her eyes. She raised an arm to shade them and blinked furiously to clear the spots out.

"Alice?" said a voice.

It was Reginald's voice.

She lowered her arm. The light had come from the brightness of the moon shining through an unclosed window; she was standing in the dining-room in front of the fireplace and the painting that Reverend Dodgson had given her; none of it had happened. She had only been sleepwalking. Her husband stood in the doorway of the dining-room, leaning on the frame.

She felt herself take a deep breath. She smelled hearth and home: the great fireplace below the painting, full of soot and cinders and smoke; the polish that the maids had used on the mantle; the smell of old dust that worked its way into every crack and seasoned the air in the old house in which they lived, like a spice. She smelled Reginald coming toward her, the oil he used in his hair and the toilet-water he used during the day still clinging to him late at night.

She turned toward him and opened her arms to embrace him. He raised his eyebrows—they were an old married couple now, long since given up their fits of temper or affection—but entered the room and put his arms around her. She leaned against his chest and heard a ticking sound.

She closed her eyes. "Your heart. It's ticking," she said.

He patted himself and pulled a watch out of the pocket of his gown. "Only because I had to check the time once I noticed you gone. Can't sleep?"

She shook her head.

His eyes flicked toward the painting. "That painting again. It draws you here often, doesn't it?"

"Only when I can't sleep," she said peevishly.

He grinned. "I know a cure for that. As long as we're both awake, that is. And we are."

She shook her head with a half-curl of a smile on her lips: she knew herself to be awake, but she couldn't make herself believe it.

"Not in the mood, eh?"

"Not quite. Perhaps closer toward morning, if I still can't sleep."

"Closer toward morning?" he asked. "Have you seen out a window?"

She looked again; the moon had vanished, and had been replaced by that particular color of hesitant gray at the horizon that meant that the sunrise would come soon.

"It's later than I realized," she admitted. A yawn came out of her throat like a large, irresistible bubble. She caught it in one hand, then stretched. "I had the most peculiar dream earlier."

"Rabbits again?"

It was a kind of code between them: "Yes…"

Reginald grunted, and waved her toward the door. "The servants'll be up soon. If nothing else, let's flee for the bedroom and spare them the sight of their betters lounging about in their nightclothes."

She began to follow him—why not?—but hesitated. In the distance, the bells of their church had begun to ring. What was the name of the services the medieval monks had held at dawn? Matins? Vespers? Lauds?

Whatever it had been called, the monks would have risen from their tasks, summoned to prayer: they were wakened before dawn, had already prayed once during the depths of the night (what *was* that called?) as if it were only their prayers that had brought the sun 'round again after all that darkness—but no, that would have been arrogant. Weren't the monks supposed to have been practicing humility?

She gave herself a little shake. She was distracting herself.

"Alice? Are you coming?"

She looked over at her husband, still holding the pocketwatch in his hand. She felt an antipathy toward the watch, and wanted it to be as far away from her as possible. An unreasonable thought, but there it was: the watch reminded her of death.

She yawned again, this time forcing the yawn out of her jaws until a real one took over. "In a moment."

"Saying goodnight to your rabbits?"

"I suppose I must," she said. "I must kiss them all on their little noses, and I don't like you to watch."

He chuckled again and left the room, taking the faint sound of the watch with him. She sighed; her shoulders dropped and her fists unclenched.

That watch! She couldn't get over the feeling that she should have liked to snatched it out of Reginald's hand and smashed it against the back of the fireplace!

She looked at the picture again; it was a watercolor of Tom Quad in early summer, the grass green and the fountain in the center of the two crossed walks flowing with sparkling water.

She leaned forward, as if she really were about to kiss the painting: the water in the fountain seemed to be moving.

The bells had ceased to ring; now it was time for all the faithful to begin their dawn prayers. A painful lump rose in her throat: if she had not denied Reverend Dodgson, admittedly no Savior, before dawn three times, then at least she had denied him once, and it filled her with hot shame.

Perhaps she owed him something after all. Some small little thing.

She put both hands against the frame, put her bare foot on a carved decoration in the fireplace, and heaved herself upward.

The Red Queen ran through the tunnels under the great plate of the Master Chronometer along with the other Wonderlandian slaves. Their feet did not march in time, but pattered like a wild storm's rainfall against a window.

She wondered what they would encounter at the far end of the tunnel: victory, defeat—or a trap. If she had tried to go back, she would have been crushed flat by the others running behind her. Twice already she had felt something underfoot that could only have been mangled clockwork.

Who drove them? Who ruled?

She found that she didn't much care, except that it was not her, and should have been.

What would they do when they arrived, assassinate the Crown? Destroy the Mainspring? Torture the courtiers? She did not like being driven through this dark metallic corridor, taking turns according to a plan that was not her own.

They were to attack the Crown, her long-time correspondent, because a winding-beetle had whispered to her that the Crown was corrupt.

Without the Crown, what would they do?

Why, they would replace him, with some noble and pure soul who would accept its obligation only reluctantly, with obvious grace. Why not? *She* had seen such events engineered before, usually by the Knave of Hearts.

Was *he* behind all this?

As little as she liked to, she kept coming back to the White Rabbit: a Wonderlandian who was able to travel from daylit to moonlit Wonderland, by joint permission of her court and the Golden Court; excused from his duties (and then arrested for performing them). The only other creature who had been given such permission was Alice.

Alice, whom the Red Queen had helped to rescue only a few moments ago, before they entered the tunnel; *Alice*, who was in truth a Wonderlandian.

The March Hare must have known: he had gone to get her, just as he had promised that he could.

And yet…

Any other Wonderlandian *but the White Rabbit* would have come unwound, to have gone to England. It was simply too far. How, then, had the March Hare fetched Alice, except that he had not fetched the true Alice at all?

And…only an Alice made of clockwork would have stayed so young, a child. The Red Queen *knew* this, she *knew* that ordinary children grew up, they did not remain the same for ever—but she had forgotten it.

Had been kept too busy to remember.

So: the March Hare was in on the plot, at the very least.

Who else?

Within the Central Palace of the Golden Court, the floors were beginning to rumble. The courtiers looked askance at each other: the elegant gold wasps, the delicate yet deadly silver damsel flies, the bronze ant-collectives, each one made up of a thousand miniature metal insects, each with its own eyes and antennae.

On its throne, which was made out of a piece of carved ruby, the Crown gnawed on its fist.

It had long known that there were plots against the Master

Chronometer, although it had not known who was responsible for them, and so it had set a subtle field around the Master Chronometer, that would strip off any minor fields of illusion that it should encounter.

Thus it had long since received the report that Alice, the mortal girl, was nothing but clockwork.

Had the Red Queen lied to him about the girl?

He could not imagine it so. She was too proud: if there had been a way for her to escape her nightly imprisonment as one of the slaves of the Master Chronometer, she would have done so without dissemble or delay. And that she was such a fool as to support the Great Unwinding, he could not countenance.

She was loud, yes, and unpleasant—but she only pretended to be a fool.

As for the White Rabbit, he remained imprisoned in his cell at the top of the tower—the part of him that had not been ground up by the gears, that was. He had been arrested at the Crown's behest, because—despite the Red Queen's assurances that the White Rabbit could never turn traitor—there was no one else who could *be* the traitor, no one else who had had access to all the secrets that had been told in his presence.

The Mainspring was nearly unwound to the point of failure and could not last the day…the moon had touched the edge of the horizon…the other side of the world was almost burning with the expected sunrise…

The Crown had no more ideas: it was time for the White Rabbit to be executed.

He hadn't the slightest idea who to trust; therefore, he would proceed with events and see who attempted to disrupt them. *Someone* was sure to try to save the poor creature, surely.

The Crown stood from its throne and said, "Bring me the head of the White Rabbit. It is time for the execution."

The courtiers thrummed with anticipation; a pair of guard quickly threw paper-scissors-stone and marched toward the tower where the White Rabbit was being kept.

The Crown seated himself, and the conversations between the members of the court resumed, first as a soft murmur, then as incessant, buzzing chatter.

Who among them was a traitor?

He had depended too much upon the Red Queen. Her plans had seemed sensible at first: establish spies among the Wonderlandians, discover what plans were set against the Mainspring, use the White Rabbit to coordinate.

They had discovered a plot known as *The Great Unwinding*, whose zealot followers believed that only in the destruction of the Mainspring would they become free of enslavement to it. Enslavement! The daylit Wonderlandians knew nothing of enslavement—their bodies did not, in the daylit hours, become part of the machine itself. The daylit Wonderlandians resented the affixing of metal plates to their mouths so that they could not speak—the moonlit

Wonderlandians could not even *think*, for their very gears became part of the Great Chronometer all day long.

If the Red Queen had known the truth, the Crown would have long since been assassinated, he had no doubt—it was he who had brokered this peace among the moonlit Wonderlandians, who hated the daylit side with a passion that they never revealed in front of them: thus the daylit Wonderlandians would march on their wheels and belts, and turn their screws and handles, and have their mouths sealed, and the moonlit Wonderlandians would not pull them gear from gear.

It was a good system, that had kept peace between daylit and moonlit sides—until now.

But then this *Great Unwinding* movement had arisen—no doubt among the selfish daylit Wonderlandians—and it had gone all wrong. Even the Red Queen had gone mad, in her plan to bring Alice to Wonderland and see what kind of trouble she stirred up. They had *nothing*, no answer as to their leaders, and no answer as to how to stop the failure of the Mainspring.

The Crown shifted in its seat; whoever had built the ruby throne had not considered the wisdom of building a throne made of a material known for its lack of friction (and thus its use in watch bearings). He was forever uncomfortably sliding about.

The time for a measured response to the threat of the saboteurs against the Mainspring and the Great Chronometer had come to an end. It was time for an ugly, but necessary, solution.

The Crown waved one hand toward his chief-of-dials, the leader of his armies, the Ante-Meridian. Sir Meridian was a curious figure, one of the military ant-collectives of the court, made of a thousand tiny brass creatures formed into the shape of a larger one: an army ant.

Sir Meridian approached the throne and performed an obeisance, lowering its multi-ant "head" to the brass plate underfoot.

"Your Majesty?"

"The time has come. You may implement Operation Daylit Saving Time."

Sir Meridian bowed even lower. "Yes, your Majesty." The several ants making up Sir Meridian burst in all directions and went their separate ways, carrying the message with them. The figure of Sir Meridian seemed to melt away down tiny messenger-tunnels around the throne.

The eyes of the court followed the event but made no comment; making note of the separation of a general or lieutenant into its component ants was considered gauche.

The Crown waited until the ants were gone, then gestured to his spymaster, who had only just returned to the court from its travels on the daylit side, and had returned in a *foul* temper, having been much abused by the clockwork Alice. "*Where* is the head of the White Rabbit? It should have been here some time ago."

"I shall find out, Your Majesty."

The spymaster's case was scratched, its arms pointing nearly upright in its annoyance. The Crown waved it back. "A moment, if you will."

"Your Majesty?"

The Crown waved the spymaster up onto the dais, then closer still. "The Alice that tortured you so, my dear cousin, has turned out to be nothing but a daylit Wonderlandian after all. She crossed onto the Great Chronometer some time ago. The anti-illusion field worked perfectly, and removed her guise as well as put her to work. The only sad news is that she is now lost among all those other daylit Wonderlandians. I can never tell them apart."

The Pocket-Watch said, "Which Alice?"

"Which Alice?"

"I explained, Your Majesty. There were two Alices; one was a small girl, and the other a grown woman. The girl I was guiding back to the Golden Court as you instructed. The grown woman was the one who tortured me: she tried to *drown* me…"

"But you cannot be harmed by water," the Crown said. "Certainly not after all *you've* been through."

"Indeed, your Majesty. But *she* did not know that. And, as I'm sure I've told you, it hurts like the devil, having water dumped into one's works like that. Or cherry juice," he added darkly.

"Two Alices," the Crown murmured. His gears were spinning,

as well they might. "Perhaps the proper Alice has come after all. Whatever happened to her?"

"I left her in the Garden, your Majesty," said his cousin, the Pocket-Watch. "She was lost in the border between Yesterday and What-Might-Have-Been, and without me to guide her, I doubt that she will ever find her way out."

Alice Hargreaves stepped through the painting and into a place that made her catch her breath—a great plain made of brass topped by a mechanical city that rose into the clouds overhead: clouds that were beginning to be lit by the earliest rays of light threading through the east, or whatever direction the sun rose in Wonderland.

She had stepped into a battlefield.

Brass figures of all shapes and sizes made of clockwork were taking up parts of the mechanical city and smashing them—unscrewing, bending, twisting, flattening, even *tearing* the metal apart. In return, enameled green metal monsters that looked like beetles half-changed into men were attacking the plain brass figures with all sorts of wrenches and hammers and screw-drivers.

The noise was deafening, but strange—neither the plain brass figures nor the green beetles said a word, nor roared or neighed or brayed or meowed or barked or even grunted.

She glanced back.

The other side of the picture-frame had disappeared, if it ever had been there at all. She was on her own, standing on top of a brass cylinder with a small gear at the top, which turned a flywheel attached to a pin. A set of delicate stairs led down off the top of the cylinder and into the chaos.

The rays of the sun had just touched the top of the tallest spire in the highest part of the mechanical city. The spire seemed impossibly tall, reaching so far up into the sky that surely it must have caught in the clouds, or even upon the moon. A bright golden line moved down the very top of the shaft, glittering in the dawn light.

As for the brass figures, their *mouths* had been bolted over with pieces of metal, so that they could not speak.

This must be the rebellion that was the Great Unwinding. It was horrible.

They could not speak…and so they destroyed that which kept them alive. They had been enslaved; they destroyed that which imprisoned them, and they would destroy themselves in the end.

Yet she could not blame them for doing so.

The sunlight lowered along the shaft of the tower.

What would happen when it reached the rest of the city?

And what would happen to the combatants?

The footsteps descending the tower steps were joined by another pair.

The White Rabbit's excellent ears pricked upward.

The pace of both sets of footsteps increased—then stopped. Banging and crashing echoed up the steps. A mighty battle! Left, right, left right!—until one of the two combatants gave a terrible metallic scream, as if it had been twisted to the point of breaking—and gone clattering and clanging down the stairs.

After a short pause, the footsteps resumed.

The light inside the cell had brightened considerably; the sun was shining on the outer wall of the tower. Steadily it approached his resting place on the floor.

What would happen when it reached him, now that he no longer bore his safe-conduct, the pocket-watch?

He continued to wait as the footsteps climbed higher and higher, and the sunlight dragged across the floor toward him. Which would arrive first? Would either arrive at all?

Louder…louder…the footsteps seemed like the tick of a slow clock.

Helplessly, the White Rabbit began to gnash his teeth.

Late, late, late, he snarled to himself.

The first group of daylit Wonderlandians had reached the end of the tunnel, which opened out onto a brass canyon that separated them from the Central Palace by four slender bridges, which they must cross to reach the Mainspring.

The Red Queen had run along with the others; now she climbed past a pair of waddling brass hedgehogs—even without their flesh they could be nothing else—and onto a slowly-spinning flywheel that rose above the heads of the crowd.

All across the plateau, other rebels were climbing out of tunnel openings hidden here and there. As of yet, none of them had dared to cross their bridges. On the other side of the canyon stood the moonlit Wonderlandians' army: the beetles in all their variety, the wasps, the crickets, the fleas: all were prepared to receive them.

The leaders of the Great Unwinding, if any, seemed to have abandoned the daylit Wonderlandians. Of the winding-beetles with their loose spirals written in cherry juice on their hidden gears, none were to be seen.

The sunlight was lowering along the tower in the center of the Central Palace. Soon, they would all be returned to the daylit side, and they would be unable to take any action at all.

They had been betrayed from within: the March Hare for certain, and…

…and the Mad Hatter, who was the March Hare's closest confidante, who had told the White Rabbit of so many of the rumors of the Great Uprising. And who had brought her…

…the Watch.

Not just any watch, no. The Pocket-Watch was the Crown's cousin. It had served as a safe-conduct for the White Rabbit, and had gone with him everywhere he went.

And heard everything that *he* had heard.

The *Watch* had been the traitor. Had heard all the secrets, had been present for all the plans.

The Watch, the March Hare, the Mad Hatter…

…all traitors.

Where were the three of them now? The Hatter she would not have recognized, not without his hat, but the March Hare, surely…with those ears…

A clatter of metal rose up from behind them, a rapid, excited banging. The Red Queen looked over her shoulder to see what was the matter.

Behind them had risen a second army, larger by far than that of the first: but these were not the noble armies of beetles and wasps, no; these were the roaches, the centipedes, the maggots.

A sneak attack. They were surrounded. Already the roaches had begun their attack, swarming over the rear of their rebel army.

Why? Why raise a rebellion only to annihilate it?

Because the daylit Wonderlandians were not necessary. Had *never* been necessary. And now they would be eradicated, for the useless nonsense that they were. Or for some other reason entirely: really, it didn't matter.

It was enough of enough.

Whatever the original purpose of the rebellion had been, *she* was done with it. Now it was hers.

She leaned down from the flywheel and plucked one of the quills of the hedgehog below her, then slid the thin stiletto of metal underneath the plate covering her mouth.

If the moonlit Wonderlandians had ever been honest, then the daylit Wonderlandians would have been allowed to *speak*.

She slid the blade all the way through, then twisted the ends together, scratching her hands severely. Fortunately, it didn't hurt. When she had finished, she stole another of the quills, twisted it into a hook, and fastened it around a spoke of the flywheel, which was so heavy that it was unlikely to be budged by what she had in mind.

Having accomplished that, she threw herself off the flywheel and dangled in midair.

The Wonderlandians around her shivered and clattered in surprise.

She held out her hands. When no one took them, she snapped her fingers imperiously, then held them out again.

A hand took one side, a claw the other.

She pulled as hard as she could against them. The rivets on either side of her mouth began to give.

She pulled harder, shaking her head from side to side as best she could, to try to loosen the rivets more.

The Wonderlandians pulled on her harder—suddenly, *much* harder. The plate began to give, the metal to bend…

A gigantic heave seemed to loosen the joints of her shoulders, and the metal groaned! The rivets rang free, pinging off the Wonderlandians around her.

She flew backward into the crowd.

They could not cheer for her, so she pushed the helping hands away and climbed back atop the flywheel and raised one fist in the air. "Wonderlandians! Wonderlandians! If you love the day, show me!"

Around her, the brass bodies raised their fists. Tentatively, their heads turning back and forth to see if anyone else was doing the same, but raising them nonetheless.

"Wonderlandians! I am your Red Queen! I am the soul of violence and retribution! Raise your fists with me! We have been duped and betrayed by the March Hare and the Mad Hatter and the Pocket-Watch, maybe others! The moonlit Wonderlandians wish us dead! But we will not die quietly before the dawn takes us home! We will fight!"

More fists rose in the air.

"We are surrounded by our enemies! What they destroy we shall rebuild! If they attack us we will *fight!*"

The Wonderlandians around her banged their arms against the gears.

In a fit of inspiration, she cried, "We will destroy their Golden Court! We will take moonlit *and* daylit Wonderland!"

The banging became louder still.

It was madness, but that had never stopped her yet.

She pointed at some of the Wonderlandians nearest the bridge. "Those of you near the bridges—begin to cross. Hold on to the metal, for they shall surely try to cut the other side. You—" she pointed toward some more of her subjects. "You begin to tear down the gears nearest you. Spears and shields! You—" she pointed toward a small spring, "Tear that down and begin unwinding it. We will need some way to drag the bridges back up the other side.

You there, begin climbing down the wall; we must find a way across the chasm below…"

She continued giving orders. They were used to obeying her, for fear of their heads. Now they obeyed her, for anger and pride and hatred and fear of once again being made slaves the next sunset.

Other Wonderlandians were getting their mouth-plates pried off. She recruited them as messengers and began sending them into the crowd to tell the ones who could not hear her: *We have been betrayed. We will fight. We will take the Golden Court and make it our own.*

Have heart.

Alice Hargreaves saw the army of pot-metal roaches swarming out of tunnels behind the clockwork Wonderlandians and began shouting to try to warn them. This plan worked excellently well—so excellently that, in fact, the roaches between her and the Wonderlandians *also* heard her, and turned to attack or capture her.

She said a quiet word of self-reproach and began to look around for something or someone that might assist her.

There was…nothing.

The Wonderlandians below her had been smashed to bits; likewise the green-enameled beetles that they had been fighting. There were no clever hiding places that the roaches would not see her go into, and pull her back out of again.

If she surrendered, she wondered, would that do any good at all?

The roaches found a Wonderlandian struggling to escape and ripped it to pieces as they marched.

…Probably not.

Alice had always been the first to enter a fight with anyone, boy or girl, when she had been younger; her boys had taken advantage of her sanguine disposition more than once to egg her on to joining their pretend battles in the nursery.

She had pretended it a bore, but had been disappointed when they had stopped.

She *would* fight.

She climbed down from the brass barrel she had been on and picked up a large piece of green armor, strapping it round her chest with a bit of spring across her shoulders. Then she picked up a beetle claw and brandished it a few times: it was long and sharp, shaped like a scimitar with an extra point in the center.

It would do.

"Never surrender! Always go down fighting!"

It was her sons' battle cry. As she shouted it, she felt tears on her cheeks—not for the smashed Wonderlandians—but for her children. For her memories of romping with them through their jungles, their mountains, their lion-filled plains, *their* Wonderlands.

She was smiling.

—

A little brass girl made out of clockwork snagged a bit of wire as she ran, and forced it underneath the horrible, awful plate that covered her mouth.

She had always thought of herself as a person; finding out that she was a piece of clockwork rather than a little girl had come to her as a bit of a shock, "but then," she thought to herself, "at least I won't have to read sermons." And when she came to think upon it, she realized that she had no memories from before the sunny afternoon on the riverbank: only memories of memories, which were like made-up stories that one had been told so many times that one thought they were actually true.

Even if they weren't.

She looped the wire around one of the metal rivets on the plate holding her mouth shut and began to worry at it. Really, it had been unnecessary to bolt her mouth shut; a stern look would have done as well…for a little while, at least.

The tunnel through which she ran was dark, only dimly lit by small lights sprinkled along the walls here and there. One of them was low enough for her to reach; she snatched it up as she ran by. It wriggled in her hand: it was a bug, a glow-bug!

She stepped into a branch of the tunnel that was quite dark. The glow-bug lit up the tunnel as it buzzed its wings and kicked its legs, trying to escape.

She waggled a finger at it, then pinned it under her foot. Whenever it struggled, she stepped on it more firmly, until it was cowed but not broken.

Then she began to worry at the rivets with the wire. A little practice and she was able to pop them out, one by one, by looping the wire directly underneath the heads of the rivets. They went pinging along the side-tunnel as the daylit Wonderlandians marched and marched and marched down the dimly-lit tunnel.

"They probably don't even know that they're being led by the glow-bugs," the clockwork girl said to herself, when she was finally able to speak aloud, having tossed the brass plate across her mouth onto the floor.

Then she picked up the glow-bug, shook it until its antennae rattled, and said, "Who's going to take me to the Crown by the straightest route before it gets its legs twisted off?"

The glow-bug writhed in her hand. The little clockwork girl gave it another shake: after finding out that she wasn't a person at all and that her home was doomed—for if she wasn't a person, where else would she have to go but Wonderland?—she had become quite ruthless.

The sound of footsteps had grown almost deafeningly loud, or else the White Rabbit had become quite afraid of them as they slowly trod their way upwards, which made them seem louder than they were. His ears trembled.

The leading edge of sunlight had almost reached him.

The top of a head appeared at the edge of one of the stairs: it was covered with light-brown curls of hair which had begun to turn to steel—no, not steel, to gray. Whoever was coming up the stairs was a *person*, made of flesh, and people made of flesh didn't have metal in their hair—the White Rabbit must remember to make a memorandum on the subject, if ever he got his body back.

The head gave a lurch upward, and a face appeared.

"Oh, my," said the White Rabbit, for he had recognized the face. It was none other than the one belonging to Reverend Dodgson.

He had a calm, wry face, with two red spots high on his cheeks from having climbed such a long way upward.

"Halloo," said the Reverend Dodgson. "I suppose you've been waiting there for quite a long time."

The White Rabbit was unable to respond, he was so overcome: Reverend Dodgson was rumored to have switched places with one of the clockwork Wonderlandians, who had gone to England in his place, but hardly anyone had seen him, either on the daylit or moonlit sides.

Reverend Dodgson reached into the pocket of his coat and pulled out a set of keys, which jingled merrily. He selected one of them as he climbed the remaining stairs, and put it in the lock.

The lock-works, the White Rabbit noticed, were moving inside the lock-plate, so that the gears inside would have jammed with any other key—but as the barrel and teeth of the key that Reverend Dodgson inserted into the lock were also moving, there was only a slight *clinkity clinkity clink* as the lock-pins and key-teeth found each other and fell into place.

Reverend Dodgson opened the door, repocketed the keys, and stooped down to pick up the White Rabbit's head, carefully holding him under the chin.

The sunlight spilled over the edge of the window, and covered the place where the White Rabbit had been resting.

"There, there," Reverend Dodgson said. "The sunlight sha'n't catch you; you may cease your shivering."

"But…Reverend Dodgson," said the White Rabbit. And then he did not know what else to say. "But…but…!"

Reverend Dodgson pulled the door of the cell closed and smiled down at him; from the White Rabbit's position in Reverend Dodgson's hands, the Reverend Dodgson's face looked immense, covered in tired old wrinkles and the slightest bit of stubble along his upper lip.

Reverend Dodgson swayed suddenly, and the White Rabbit almost slipped from his grip. The White Rabbit, who felt as though he were being juggled, closed his eyes to keep the room from spinning.

"Oh," said the Reverend Dodgson.

"What is it?"

"I must rest, Mister Rabbit, for I am quite old."

The White Rabbit spat out, "But Wonderland is in terrible danger! The Mainspring…there are plots to have it unwound…and then where shall we be? Are you here to save us?"

Reverend Dodgson shook his head. "I am dying, Mister Rabbit."

And before the White Rabbit could recover from the shock of that statement, Reverend Dodgson added, "And before I do, I would like to accomplish something that I should have done a long time ago. Pray chance, do you happen to know where I might find the watch that you have been carrying about? Not the one that is in your drawer in your cottage at home, but the one that you were more recently given by the Crown as a safe-conduct against the rising and setting of the moon?"

The White Rabbit frowned. "I am afraid it was either taken from me, sir, or else lost, when I was arrested. I am sorry of it; the Pocket-Watch was a good and faithful companion."

One of Reverend Dodgson's eyebrows twitched.

"Where did it come from before then?" he asked. "Before it was given to you as a companion?"

"Why, from the Golden Court," the White Rabbit said. "It is the cousin of the Crown, you know. They are quite similar in appearance—"

Reverend Dodgson interrupted him, saying, "Then we shall descend the tower stairs and see whether we can find him there, in the Court. For the Pocket-Watch that accompanied you about Wonderland is no faithful companion: it is the companion of the March Hare and the Mad Hatter, who are behind the plot to destroy Wonderland with the Great Unwinding."

The White Rabbit gasped in horror, but Reverend Dodgson only turned and began descending the stairs at a slow, steady rate.

"Oh, hurry, hurry!" cried the White Rabbit.

"No need," said Reverend Dodgson. "We are caught in between moon-set and sun-rise for as long as need be now, perfectly balanced—and we shall stay here until one of two things happens."

"What…er…are those?" the White Rabbit asked.

"Either I am able to do what must be done, or else I first expire," answered the Reverend Dodgson. "For the Mainspring has just given out, proper Wonderland time has stopped, and the Great Unwinding has begun."

The Crown said, with a mounting annoyance: "Where *is* the White Rabbit? What has caused this additional delay?"

The members of the Court had gone to the windows of the throne room in order to watch the combat going on outside. The army that surrounded the Central Palace was made up of crack troops; the second army, which surrounded the rebelling Wonderlandians from behind, was made up of lesser troops but in greater numbers: ones which would crush the daylit Wonderlandians like a stone being smashed into clockwork. Indelicate but sure.

The Crown regretted the destruction of the daylit Wonderlandians, but there was no other way to ensure that traitors were no longer in their midst. It had to be done, for the good of all.

The Pocket-Watch had hurried off to the tower to discover what had happened; in a moment he was running back as quickly as his short legs would allow, his face much distressed.

The Crown rose to his feet; only the escapements in his working kept his hands from spinning 'round the dial, he was suddenly so afraid.

"Your Majesty, your Majesty!" cried the Watch.

The courtiers at the window seemed to notice nothing, they were so engrossed in the sights occurring outside the palace.

The floor seemed to vibrate, then. It was not so much movement as it was sound—the sound of something that had stopped.

"The Mainspring—!" whispered the Crown.

The Watch seemed not to have noticed. It continued running toward him, approaching the throne and giving a quick curtsy. "The watch-beetle that I sent to bring back the White Rabbit has been smashed, your Majesty! I fear that the conspirators have made their way into the Central Palace!"

The Crown said, "You fool. It is worse than that. The Mainspring has stopped."

The eyes of the Pocket-Watch, made of clouds, stretched wider open for a moment, then turned to narrow slits.

"Then," the Pocket-Watch said, "your usefulness is at an end, Cousin Crown. Once I have dismantled you, I shall be able to sit on your throne and take your place as the gear that guides the Mainspring. *I will be able to rework the Master Chronometer itself,* an opportunity that you wasted!"

The Crown felt a thin sliver of metal slide into his gears from behind, jamming them.

"Cousin…" he gasped. "I am…only a gear…no power…"

"You lie!" cried the Pocket-Watch. "In the moments between your destruction and all of Wonderland becoming unwound, my allies will take your mainspring and replace my own with it—*and then I shall be the last power in Wonderland.*"

In the few ticks that he had left, the Crown grimaced.

"It is not…my…mainspring…which holds the last…"

He closed his eyes for a moment. He was weakening, his face going numb, his hands limp. He turned to see who had stabbed him—and found that the throne itself had stood upright behind him, and shoved a piece of heavy wire into his gears.

"Et tu, Pulvinus…"

He fell forward into the arms of the Pocket-Watch, his gears jammed and consciousness fading…

—

The Red Queen watched the first bridge rise across the chasm: the bridges that had once crossed the gap had all been cut down, soon after the attack had begun. But enough of the daylit Wonderlandians had climbed down the wall of the chasm, then climbed up the other side, that they were able to protect a small part of the Mainspring for a short while against the Crown's troops. A new bridge was quickly raised, then reinforced: a wave of troops charged across it, even climbed along the bottom, upside-down.

The Red Queen noted with satisfaction that the bridge would hold, and her troops would be able to defend it—then turned away.

Behind them, the Wonderlandians rallied against the army of rusty roaches and the other common foot soldiers of the Crown's army. These low troops did not fight as well as her daylit Wonderlandians; *her* troops had had a daily taste of freedom, and fought for the rest of it; the roaches fought only as much as was necessary for their masters not to beat them. They were slaves.

And so the rear of her army was holding its position as well.

She had a number of units searching for additional tunnel entrances, so that they could not be surprised from within—and more units searching the known tunnels, trying to find a hidden way across to the Central Palace.

Soon they would have a second bridge in place, and a third—and when the third bridge had been raised, she would lead the main body of her army across them, to meet the enemy's forces on the other side.

Her victory was assured. And yet…

The sun had stopped in the sky.

She had eyes watching the skies in case of aerial attack; she had internal units watching out for spies and traitors; she used her own eyes to overlook her troops, watching for surprises. Still the sensation that she was missing a possible line of attack bothered her.

With the sun unexpectedly at a halt, they had the time they needed to attack: the dawn lingered, preventing them from being transported back to the daylit Wonderland— where they were free, but unable to secure that freedom when next the sun set.

She did not know why the sun had stopped, but she would take what advantage from it she could.

The second bridge arose, along with a cheer. The bridge in the center, the widest of the three, was being dragged up by daylit Wonderlandians even as the troops of the Crown threw barbs and pins down at the climbers below. Two wings of the daylit armies poured across the bridges, swinging toward the center bridge, clearing a path as they charged.

The Red Queen looked back over her shoulder, and raised a hand in signal, holding a polished gear in her hand. The army behind her began falling back toward her, in preparation of moving across the bridges. When they had crossed, they would collapse what they had built, and leave what was left of the roach army on the other side. No doubt the roaches would swarm down into the cavern between the gears and the Mainspring, but they would have to slow in order to do so.

They would lose time…

The third bridge was up!

The advance guard charged across it—it held!

Eager hands helped lift the Red Queen down from the tallish flywheel where she had been standing, and she joined the center of a tight phalanx of warriors—loyal cardsmen, their flat bodies unmistakable.

She raised a mace made of a discombobulated gear. "Charge!"

The little clockwork girl dashed through the pitch-black tunnels, keeping her hands positioned around the glow-bug's neck and abdomen, so that she could twist off its head at a moment's notice if need be. It had misled her once, and in return she had stretched its neck out so that the little gears inside could be seen turning frantically. After that incident, it had led her in a more or less straight line—one that had worked steadily downwards.

Now they were racing underneath a *very* low ceiling, and the tunnel around them sang with a low, groaning sound, one that was almost too low of the clockwork girl's ears to hear.

"What is that, I wonder," said the clockwork girl.

The glow-bug, not being able to speak, did not answer. The clockwork girl almost pitied the creature—not that *that* would have prevented her from torturing it again.

The noise stopped mid-groan; the clockwork girl stumbled on her feet and had to lean against the wall of the tunnel, as she came to a shuddering stop.

"I feel rather queer," she said. She was not used to feeling like a piece of clockwork, so she did not know whether she felt queer because she did not feel like a little girl, or because her clockwork had gone wrong.

The glow-bug seemed to agree: its glow flickered unsteadily.

The clockwork girl forced herself to keep walking through the tunnel, hunched over so that she did not hit her head. "It can't be far now."

It was not: ahead of them only a short way was the opening to a narrow set of stairs, that went 'round and 'round in circles. Just inside the stairway was a heavy, windowless, locked brass door: the keyhole seemed as though it were also a winding-gear socket, as though the gears inside the door must be wound if they were to open.

The glow-bug kicked its legs as if to remind her that it *might* be released, now that there was some other light.

The clockwork girl gripped it tighter, using her hand to cover the glowing part of the bug's body, which was a kind of glass vial filled with chemicals. Now it was quite dark in the stairway. The clockwork girl began climbing the stairs again, as quietly as she was able, which was not very quietly at all.

Her footsteps echoed up the stairs: the silence surrounding her made her gears chatter.

The Pocket-Watch let the Crown slide out of his arms and onto the floor of the Golden Court, changing his face to match the Crown's as he did so.

The Mainspring had stopped but the tick of the last gears in the Master Chronometer had not: the secret store of energy that the Pocket-Watch had thought reserved inside of the Crown had not been that which powered the machinery of Wonderland, not at all.

The Crown was nothing but a glorified winding-stem after all.

The true power of Wonderland lay elsewhere.

The Pocket-Watch waddled over to one of the guards, snatched its spear—a watch case opener on a long metal rod—went back to his cousin and began dismantling him, piece by piece.

Just to be sure. He pulled out the Crown's mainspring and shook it: dead, dead as a door-nail.

The guards gaped at him. The Pocket-Watch snarled: "That damned cousin of mine, the Pocket-Watch, is a traitor. He must be removed. See to it."

The guards snapped to attention, then began crossing the throne room.

—

Alice Hargreaves fought the roaches, denting them, shouting at them, and generally scaring them off, until she was suddenly grabbed from behind and dragged along: at first she resisted with all her might, but then a voice purred in her ear, "If you're trying to make mock-turtle soup, shouldn't you get a bowl or a pot first?"

Alice started in surprise: a weight had settled on her shoulder, soft, furred, and heavy.

A cat floated above her shoulder—but only the head. The rest of the cat had gone invisible, even if she could feel its tail curl around the side of her neck. The Cheshire Cat.

She twisted 'round and saw that a Wonderlandian with an enormous brass shell on its back was trying to drag her to safety: a small phalanx of warriors had broken through the admittedly soft roach army lines in order to save her.

The Wonderlandians were in retreat.

"Oh, no," she said.

The Cheshire Cat said, "Oh, yes. I went to the top of the tower and looked down to see what I could see. And do you know what I saw? I saw a clockwork figure who looked a great deal like the Red Queen charging across the bridge to the Mainspring and the Central Palace of the Golden Court, which is where you wanted to go in the first place, is it not?"

Alice got her feet up underneath her and gave a quick curtsy to the clockwork turtle, delivering her apologies and thanks at nearly the same time.

Then she whispered to the Cat, "Are you animal, mineral, or vegetable?"

"I am all three," stated the Cat proudly. "But if you would like to know whether I am clockwork or not, then yes, I am—the sunlight touched me and liberated my tongue as well as returned my fur to its most comfortable, if somewhat mussed, disposition. But it did not whisk me back to the daylit side, which I found curious. Do you not?"

"I…find it curious as well," Alice said, untangling the meaning of the Cat's words as quickly as she could. The phalanx of clockwork warriors was pushing through the crowds of other daylit Wonderlandians, clanking their forelimbs together as they jogged.

"Most curious," said the Cat. "Time appears to have stopped."

"What about the Mainspring?"

The Cat leaned close to her ear and whispered in a low voice nearly drowned out by the sounds of the phalanx marching and beating their limbs together. "Word to the wise. Don't mention that word where anyone else might hear you."

"The Mainspring? Why?"

"Didn't I just say not to mention it?"

"Isn't it too late for that?"

The Cat nipped her on the ear. "It's far too late for many things…but not for that. Hush now, for we're making such good time that we're almost across the bridge."

They had crossed the Master Chronometer almost in a breeze; Alice blinked and started—it was if they had moved in a dream.

Ahead of them was a great canyon in the metallic city: on one side, the clockwork moved and turned and clicked and danced—where it had not been wrenched apart or destroyed. On the other side, there was only a large brass barrel topped with crystal or glass, and two armies fighting upon it. The tall spire was in the center of the barrel, and around it what seemed a clockwork palace, a kind of orrery that turned 'round on itself at different speeds, revolving around the tower.

The phalanx of warriors led her across the center bridge, their feet banging in unison on the brass plates that had been wired and banded together, and that jiggled unsteadily underfoot.

"Where are we going?" The edge of the Mainspring was fast approaching.

"To the Red Queen, I should think," the Cat said. "She always considered you her secret weapon."

"I?"

"Always turning up where you were least expected or wanted, flipping over jurors, tramping over tablecloths, that sort of thing."

"If I recall," Alice said, "it was you who told me several times which direction to go."

"*I* only asked which way you would like to go," said the Cat. But it began to purr again, as if she had given it a compliment.

They crossed over the bridge and stepped onto the other side—and suddenly Alice's heart gave a lurch, and she fell forward on her hands and knees.

The Cat disappeared from her shoulder and appeared on the top of the Turtle's shell. "You remain as graceful as ever."

But Alice was looking downward through the glass to the Mainspring below: the great metal ribbons that made up the spring inside the barrel were turning—becoming looser. The loops of the spring were widening, the outer layer resting against the barrel. About three-quarters of the spring seemed to be unwound; soon, the unwinding would reach the center of the spring.

Alice opened her mouth to say something, then closed it and looked up at the Cat.

It had stood up on the Turtle's back with its tail sticking straight out and every bit of fur on its body standing on end. It gave a terrible *hissss*.

A cry was going up from the armies around them: "The Mainspring! Look!"

The fighting of the two armies stopped suddenly, as all looked through the glass that was under their feet.

Reverend Dodgson carried the head of the White Rabbit the rest of the way down the stairs; the walls 'round them seemed to buzz past at a reckless speed, even though Reverend Dodgson hardly seemed to move as he descended.

They had soon arrived at the throne room, which had become the scene of a riot. All the moonlit Wonderlandians of the Golden Court had fallen into a panic, and were trying to escape out-of-doors—too many of them had tried to fit through at the same time, and now they were jammed together.

The White Rabbit said, "However shall we escape?"

"We shall *not* escape," Reverend Dodgson said. "For this is where we ought to be."

The White Rabbit did not know how to respond to that, so he looked about the throne room as best as he was able. What he saw dismayed him.

The Crown was dead; its glass has been smashed and its face removed, its gears scattered across the floor. Small brass cleaning fleas were attempting to drag the pieces away, but they kept having to stop and sob.

The ruby throne was now occupied by the Pocket-Watch that had been the White Rabbit's companion ever since the Red Queen had asked for his, the White Rabbit's, assistance in the matter of the threats against the Mainspring and how to repair it. The Watch's face had changed so that it resembled that of its cousin, but the White Rabbit could recognize it by the scratches on its case.

He shivered.

The Pocket-Watch turned slowly in their direction, its cloud-eyes becoming slits as it spied the two of them. Reverend Dodgson remained calmly standing at the base of the tower.

"You!" said the Pocket-Watch. "What are *you* doing here? The Mainspring is stopped! Why are you not dead?"

"I *am* dying," admitted Reverend Dodgson. "But, much like a clock whose winding-stem has been ruined," he looked pointedly down at the broken Crown, "I have a few ticks left in me as I wind down."

"Guards!" the Pocket-Watch shouted. "Attack the intruders!"

This exclamation did not have the results that the usurping Watch expected; those who heard the cry of their new ruler turned, saw Reverend Dodgson, and knelt upon the brass.

"The Watchmaker, the Watchmaker," they murmured.

Reverend Dodgson raised his free hand and coughed into it. "Hardly a watchmaker," he muttered to himself. "And if I were a watchmaker, then who made me?"

A cry went up from the packed doors of the palace; the courtiers were shoved back indoors; the army of brass Wonderlandians had arrived!

After the first rows of invaders had made their way inside the Central Palace, they parted to let a short, solid figure through.

At first the White Rabbit did not recognize it, but then he noticed that the figure had appended to itself a heart-shaped gear upon its breast, as well as placed another gear 'round its head, to indicate a crown.

Being unable to bow or otherwise perform an obeisance, he lowered his eyes: the Red Queen had arrived.

Behind her was Alice.

In a white nightgown and robe that had suffered rips and tears as well as stains, the woman who had grown from little girl was not much the same. Her dark hair had grown long and lay in a mussed braid along her back; she must have grown at least two feet in height at least.

But it was *her*. The expression of arrogant mischief (whether bluffing or otherwise) had not left her face. *This* was a girl who would smash all one's furniture, or disrupt a legal proceeding; *this* was a girl who would pick one up by the tummy and shake one until one fainted.

She could destroy them all, if the whim took her: it was simply one of the rules of this place.

She walked softly upon the brass floor, making not the least sound whatsoever in her bare feet; to a creature accustomed to the constant clink of footsteps, it was unnerving.

The moonlit Wonderlandians did not know who approached; they were still in the thrall of Reverend Dodgson, carefully holding the White Rabbit's head.

"Halloo," he said. "I'm afraid Mister Rabbit has lost himself. Would anyone happen to have a spare bit of clockwork that we might use to put him back together again?"

It was an unreasonable request for an unreasonable assembly. "Really, Reverend Dodgson, that isn't—"

Reverend Dodgson put his fingers to the White Rabbit's mouth. "Hush. It *is* rather awkward carrying a rabbit's head about, you know."

In short order, the body of a daylit Wonderlandian had appeared and been set up in the throne room, and Reverend Dodgson affixed the White Rabbit's head onto the body. It did not quite work, and Reverend Dodgson was forced to remove the head and untwist a big of metal flange that had gone wrong when the White Rabbit's head had been chopped off.

"The bodies are easier to replace than the heads," Reverend Dodgson said, as he worked. "I had to make sure that the daylit Wonderlandians would be able to survive their queen, after all!"

The entire time that he tinkered with the White Rabbit's head, the daylit and moonlit Wonderlandians—as well as Alice—were forced to stand about and wait. The White Rabbit had never been so embarrassed in his life: to have to be repaired by the Watchmaker—!

"There," Reverend Dodgson said. "I believe that should do it. Dear Mister Rabbit, do take a turn around me, and let me see whether all is in order."

The White Rabbit, a furred head on a naked metal body, took his first tentative step, then another. The body was unfamiliar to him, and lurched as he tried to catch his balance. He slipped, and Reverend Dodgson caught him and lifted him back up again.

"Thank you, Reverend Dodgson."

"My pleasure."

The White Rabbit continued to walk in a circle around Reverend Dodgson, then came to a shuddering halt.

"Do you think you have it?" Reverend Dodgson asked.

"As well I might for the moment, thank you," he answered.

It was absurd. Reverend Dodgson turned to the rest of the company.

Suddenly, the White Rabbit noticed that the Pocket-Watch, still on the dais directly behind Reverend Dodgson and perhaps hidden from most of the crowd. He had twisted off one of his own face-hands and was raising it to stab Reverend Dodgson directly in the back.

"Look out!" shouted the White Rabbit.

The Pocket-Watch froze in place; tears of red fluid—cherry juice, perhaps—began to drip from the corners of his eyes.

Reverend Dodgson turned to look over his shoulder. His slight, subtle expression of mischief fell. "Ah…we have one more person to join us, I see. Do come out."

A clockwork girl stepped out from behind the throne, one fist around a glow-bug and the other holding the watch-back opener like a spear.

A wave of fruity, rich perfume rolled off the dais. The back of the Pocket-Watch fell onto the dais and rolled away, falling onto the floor and spinning like a coin.

Then the Pocket-Watch toppled forward, hitting the ground where Reverend Dodgson had been standing a moment before.

The White Rabbit breathed a sigh of relief, having just removed Reverend Dodgson two steps to the right. The

Pocket-Watch's watch-works were still strangely filled with mashed cherries, he noted. It was an impossibility that it had worked at all. He must make a memorandum to study such things, if…

The White Rabbit shook his head. That was a substantial *if* indeed.

"Hello, Reverend Dodgson," the clockwork girl said.

"My dear, er, girl," said Reverend Dodgson, giving a furtive look at the woman Alice. "How do you do?"

"I am afraid," she said simply, and for a moment the White Rabbit wondered how she might finish the sentence: *I am afraid that I am not very well; I am afraid that I've caught a bit of a bug; I am afraid that we meet under very trying circumstances.* But that was all of the sentence in its entirety.

"As am I," Reverend Dodgson said.

"I don't wish to die. Has the other Alice come here to break us?"

"I do not know," Reverend Dodgson said. "She certainly has the right to, and perhaps it would be for the best."

The woman in her braid crossed her arms over her chest and raised an eyebrow, but said nothing.

The clockwork girl looked about the room: "The Pocket-Watch was a traitor after all."

"A boojum," said Reverend Dodgson.

The clockwork girl cocked her head to the side. "I see, that is the word for it then? A boojum."

"Yes."

"I came to try to save Wonderland," the clockwork girl said. "I spoke to an Other Alice who said it was *rotten* and she wouldn't."

"Ah…" Reverend Dodgson said. "Did you travel so far from Wonderland, then? For it must have been a terrible long way to go, if you made it to the Islands of Other Times."

"I froze in place," the clockwork girl said.

"I'm sure you did."

"The Other Alice was cruel. She said that she would like to see us all smashed up, that we were a poor excuse for a Wonderland. The other one was nicer, she said."

"One mustn't trust an Alice," Reverend Dodgson said sternly. "They're temperamental."

"I'm an Alice, too, you know," the clockwork girl said in an aggrieved voice.

"I know." Reverend Dodgson stood up again, looking at all the clockworks about him. He stooped to pick up a loose gear that had belonged to the Crown. "I see that glow-bug that you have in your fist. You might as well release it."

With a metallic sigh, she opened both her hands: the bug dropped onto the floor, then quickly crawled under the dais. The watch-back opener clattered to the floor next to the Pocket-Watch.

"Reverend Dodgson," came the mortal Alice's voice from the center of the throne room. "What is the meaning of all this?"

Reverend Dodgson's hands had gone a softish gray color, almost as if the flesh underneath the skin had been replaced by metal.

He put one hand over the center of his chest.

"All of this…" Reverend Dodgson wheezed. "What. Is the meaning. Of all this."

He swayed, and the White Rabbit reached to steady him.

"The meaning," he said. "Ah, the meaning of all this." He coughed into his hand. "The meaning of all this…I am a poor man," he said. "A very poor man."

The mortal Alice looked sharply at Reverend Dodgson, then began to push through the ranks of Wonderlandians. Reverend Dodgson leaned forward and began to cough weakly into his hand.

It was the Pocket-Watch who moved first, grabbing Reverend Dodgson by his trouser-leg and pulling itself upright. Its face had gone starless and gray.

"You!" it shrieked. "It was *you* all along!"

Then it bent down, picked up the watch-back opener, and swung it directly into Reverend Dodgson's chest.

Reverend Dodgson's face went entirely gray; his mouth opened and closed like that of a beached goldfish.

The Pocket-Watch's works had fallen out of its case with the impact, along with the cherry-mash…the barrel of its mainspring burst open, and the thin strands of its spring leapt about the room, making the Wonderlandians flinch.

The White Rabbit had grabbed Reverend Dodgson tight in order to keep him from falling; now Reverend Dodgson had gone limp, and his weight began to drag them both to the floor. He lay Reverend Dodgson down as gently as he might. The man still gasped, as if for breath.

The Pocket-Watch and his various parts were dragged away by the guards.

Reverend Dodgson reached out a hand for Alice, who had just reached the two of them. He coughed weakly.

"Alice," he said. "Please…forgive me. I am dying. I lied to you…I did not want…to ask…this favor…but…"

He closed his eyes and everyone around them went still.

The White Rabbit held his breath: Reverend Dodgson's eyes must open again…

Alice took his hand for a moment and held it, pressed it against her cheek, then said, "It's cold. His hand. It's quite cold, like a piece of metal—"

She stood up, grasped Reverend Dodgson by the top of his head, braced one bare foot on the knee of his trousers, and pulled.

"You are nothing but a fraud!"

"No! Alice!" shouted the White Rabbit, a moment too late.

With a *pop* and the tearing of a silk tie, the head came loose, revealing the rotation of mechanical gears underneath.

"Reverend Dodgson!" she shouted, her voice terrible with anger. "How dare you lie to me *again*."

Then a gray circle surrounded the White Rabbit's vision, which quickly closed in until he could see nothing at all—but it did not worry him in the slightest; for he had gone completely still, so still that he could not even think.

Everyone around her seemed to freeze at once, so still that not the least sound could be heard, not even the ticking of the clock that made up the city around them.

Alice shuddered and put the head of the false Reverend Dodgson down upon the floor of the throne room. The gears inside the false Reverend Dodgson gave a short whirr, then stopped.

The last of the clockwork spring power had been used up; Wonderland was finished.

She had destroyed it after all.

AFTERWORD

Where did the *Alice in Wonderland* books end? Did they end when Reverend Dodgson was expelled, as it were, from the Liddell house? Did they end after the second book, written when Alice was altogether too grown-up and ladylike for such things?

Or did they end with the picture that the Reverend Dodgson gave Alice for her wedding to Reginald Hargreaves?

Did they end when Alice, now an adult and finally out from under her mother's thumb, failed to repair her relationship with the don? Did they end when she named her son Carryl, then denied that his naming had anything to do with her old friend?

Did they end on those nights that Alice would be unable to sleep, and would stand in front of the picture for hours, trying to work up the courage to go through?

Did they end when the Mainspring wound down, or when the false Reverend Dodgson was beheaded?

Or do they end when you close this book?

Alice stumbled out of the throne room filled with frozen clockwork: the daylit Wonderlandians, the moonlit Wonderlandians, the palace itself. She appeared to be the only one still capable of movement, or life, or thought.

The sun had resumed its path through the sky, and the rays of sun had finally begun to descend the tower in the center of the palace. The shifting shadows made it seem as though the frozen statues were moving in the corner of her eye.

She wandered the glass-topped Mainspring, looking into its depths: it was still slowly moving inside, the metal ribbons unwinding from their center slowly, then with a sudden jerk that made the ribbons swish against each other, then slowly again.

What was the meaning of all this?

She had put Reverend Dodgson on trial and found him false.

She did not wish to be here any longer, but hadn't the slightest idea of how to depart: finally she stopped where she was and waited for the sun to touch her. It didn't take long. It bathed her in golden light: and then she was gone.

—

She did not return home, but to a giant cherry tree whose branches were heavy with fruit. A court had been held there; she knew it by the wooden throne that had been grown into the trunk. Hearts had been carved into the bark: *RQ* marked the center of each.

The leaves of the tree seemed to be turning yellow—the machinery of life could be unwound, just as sure as that of a mechanical watch. The leaves rustled in the breeze and fell in a lazy golden drizzle; otherwise, the tree was silent.

Death. She had faced it often enough before: her sister Edith…her father…Reverend Dodgson…her first love, Leopold…and more, always more. Things were always becoming unwound.

Would she ever know what had happened here? Had Reverend Dodgson really switched places with a clockwork version of himself? *She* had been fooled by a clockwork version: why not all of England?

Who had been behind the plot of the Great Unwinding? The Pocket-Watch, with the help of, say, the Mad Hatter and the March Hare? Would she ever know?

She walked along the boughs of the tree, never watching where she put her feet, and yet never falling.

As the morning wore into afternoon, her stomach growled, and the leaves began to fall more quickly.

Her concerns became less philosophical and more practical: finding something to eat. Finding a way out.

—

She climbed down out of the cherry tree, her hands and mouth smeared in red. Her feet and hands were covered in blisters and splinters, and her gown was hopelessly torn.

Home…home. How would she get home? In the past she had simply awakened, once she had reversed the order of the day in Wonderland, either by becoming queen or by turning the tables of justice on the house of cards that had been the Red Queen's court.

Hadn't she done that now?

She was rapidly becoming sick of cherries, and lonely and bored. Even one of Ina's books of sermons might have done her some good.

The day continued; the cherry tree now let fall immense waterfalls of leaves that would have covered entire palaces. She wandered the island upon which the tree had grown; around it lay a perfectly round moat, with four bridges following a pair of paths that met at the trunk of the tree and crossed at right angles. She recognized it; she had been here before.

On the other side of the bridges began the hedge-labyrinth: looking down from the base of the cherry-tree, she was able to see fountains, hedges, hedge-animals, more— the Tweedles' house, with household goods slung all about the grounds; the Duchess's country-house with its door sealed and pottery everywhere; the tea-table; banquet tables and battlefields; chess squares; flower-beds; tulgey woods. All of it was folded into the labyrinth. It took less space than she would have thought—the way everything twist-ed and turned, the Forgotten Wood had been just across one of the hedges from the law-court where the Knave of Heart's trial had been held.

If she squinted, she could see the sea, crashing against a ring of white sand surrounding Wonderland: and in the hazy distance, other islands, larger or smaller—other worlds.

It was, she realized, the reverse side of the moonlit Wonderland—the cherry tree and the pinlike tower, the Mainspring and the little hill upon which the tree stood, the Master Chronometer and the labyrinth. Two sides of the same coin: or else the inside and the face of a great clock, or else some other shape which she could barely imagine.

And now it had gone all wrong, with no one to fix it.

And no way for her to escape.

She tried to lie down on the soft green grass of a clearing and sleep, but she could not. She could not sleep.

After a time, she pricked herself with a piece of wire she had saved, to see whether she could still bleed, or if she had been somehow changed with a piece of clockwork without her knowing it—like that poor little clockwork girl.

She still was able to bleed.

—

When the full moon rose and its light struck her, she went back to the moonlit lands, still fortunately as herself, and not a mechanical creature. The statues of all the Wonderlandians were still there.

In a kind of horrified daze, she replaced the false Reverend Dodgson's head on its shoulders, and turned it this way and that until it gave a *clink* and settled into place.

The false Reverend Dodgson did not come to life. It was too late to undo what she had done, to revise the book upon which she had closed the cover.

Despair settled over her like a blanket; she sat on the glass barrel of the Mainspring and stared down into the depths: the spring was almost entirely pressed out against the outer rim of the barrel. She could see smashed fragments of clockwork lying under and between the ribbons, as if something small had tried to push back against the spring and keep it from unwinding further, had failed, and been smashed.

There being nothing to eat or to drink upon the Great Chronometer, and no way to sleep, she soon found herself talking to herself:

"This is the price of curiosity, you know. You *had* to know what was on the other side of the painting. And back you are in Wonderland, or at least *a* Wonderland, for it resembles very little of the Wonderlands that I remember from before. You should be happy as anything, for now you have found what it was so maddening not to know: that Wonderland was as mad as ever, that no-one and no-thing was to be trusted, and of course that included Reverend Dodgson, and that you're a terrible person who can't leave well enough alone, and now it's all your fault: you simply *had* to find out whether Reverend Dodgson was a bit of clockwork or not. And now you know."

Even though she had been quite angry when she had thought that Reverend Dodgson had switched places with a clockwork man, abandoning him in England—and why should she have been angry, except that she felt deep in her ugly heart that remaining in England was a terrible fate— she felt all the worse now, knowing that, after all, Reverend Dodgson had been dead for some time in England, and *this* one the false coin.

She sniffed and rubbed her nose on the sleeve of her robe. She hadn't admitted it to herself before, but—she missed him.

"And you are *not* happy. You never should have come here. You should have left it a pleasant, distant memory— or even a bitter, distant memory. As long as you had kept it at arm's length, that would have been enough. *Now* you cannot go home."

She wished…she wished that her heart had not given a leap when she had said that: not to go home? Unthinkable. And yet perhaps that was the reason she had not awakened yet from the madness of the Golden Court—after she beheaded the false Reverend Dodgson, she *should* have—Wonderland should have popped like a bubble, and she should have wakened, as if from a dream.

That was the way the story went, after all.

She wished…she wished…

She did not know what she wished, although she felt herself wish it with all her heart: her heart was no bit of clockwork, to be made to wind up and turn in a regular sort of way.

She found a hand-crank among the armies of Wonderlandians on the top of the Mainspring; she took it back with her to the throne-room.

The Wonderlandians all had a socket into which the hand-crank fitted, hidden somewhere on their bodies. Alice found the false Reverend Dodgson's socket, which was on the back of his neck, and tried to wind him—but there emitted only a horrible grinding sound from within, and his head attempted to turn 'round and 'round on its shoulders. She stopped.

She considered winding the White Rabbit, but she doubted he knew more than she had guessed, or that he knew how to repair the Mainspring itself, and she thought that for once he might like to rest.

The Red Queen she might also wind—but if the Red Queen had had an answer to all of this, she would have taken advantage of it—not wasted time in leading a war that could not be won.

And so she came to the clockwork Alice, who had frozen on top of the dais from which she had prevented the Pocket-Watch from doing what the mortal Alice had done soon after. The mortal Alice inserted the hand crank into the socket on the bottom of the clockwork girl's foot, grasped the turning handle and the side handle to steady it, and began turning.

The main gear turned a smaller gear on the central shaft of the hand-crank, which turned the clockwork girl's winding-gear, which wound the girl. No grinding sounds emitted from the clockwork girl's gears—but she didn't move, either.

Not having anything better to do, Alice kept winding until finally she could feel the tension of the winding-gear fighting her: she did not wish to over-wind the girl, so Alice stopped and took away the crank.

At first, nothing happened. Then the clockwork girl opened her glassy eyes and turned them toward Alice.

"Hello," she said in a flat, mechanical voice. "You're Alice. The real one, I mean."

"I suppose I am," she said.

"If you want to destroy Wonder-land then you will have to talk to some-one else."

"I don't wish to destroy Wonderland. I only wish to go home."

"Some-times that is the same thing, I think."

Alice ignored that. "Do you know how to fix the Mainspring?"

"I think I know where the door is to get in-side. But you need a key that looks like a gear. The door is locked."

"Where is the door?"

"Near the bott-om of the stairs in the tower. The glow-bug showed me the way."

"Where might I find a key?"

"No, no, no," said the clockwork girl. "It will only take your heart. No. Nooo. Nooooo."

Her moans became distant and echoing. After a moment she went still.

Alice remembered hearing a jingling from Reverend Dodgson's pockets when she had been searching for his winding-gear. A moment later she was holding a key-ring with eight or nine keys on it.

"Like this?" she asked the clockwork girl.

But the clockwork girl had wound down.

Alice went down the stairs in the tower, 'round and 'round until she had reached the locked doorway, which looked like the door of a bank vault. She tried each of the keys in order until she found one that would fit—two of the keys were still sluggishly moving—and used it to wind the door.

The door gave a brief chime, then unlocked itself.

She opened it.

A clock ticked softly from the other room; the moon-light shone across the dining-room floor. All was as it had been: the painting, the fireplace, the moon, the doorway, the table, the sideboards, the china-cupboard, the rugs…the dust…

She had been away no time at all.

Alice ran her hands through her hair to make sure she didn't have hedge-twigs in it, only to discover that it had been cut short and felt both terribly thin and terribly coarse.

With shaking hands she brought her hands in front of her face: they were wrinkled and old, the joints swollen, the bones gone slightly crooked.

She was wrong; she had been away a *very* long time.

Her mouth was dry and her legs were weak. She wore a different robe and nightgown than she remembered; she had taken the time (this time) to put on a pair of slippers.

A mirror waited her in the hallway, to see what damage Time had done.

But first, she reached up and touched the painting. It was still warm soft to the touch, and felt as though it would only take a good, solid push for her to go through.

It did not feel of clockwork, but an old woman's cheek.

As she lowered her hand she felt a weight shifting in one pocket of her robe; she reached in and pulled out a pocket-watch. Reginald's. She turned it over and over in her hands, then lifted it to her ear: it was silent; it had gone still a long time ago, soon after his death.

She remembered.

She had sold the original manuscript then, at Sotheby's, in order to keep the house. She knew she wouldn't live for ever, and that the old ways of country-houses and squires was over: but she *would* like to live out the rest of her days in the house where she had loved Reginald for so long and raised her three boys—two of whom had died in the Great War, leaving only Carryl to carry the name.

She had no heart for anything else.

She turned the crown of the watch. It made a grinding noise; the works inside were broken. She could have sent it to be fixed but in all truth she *had* only kept it these last eight years because it had stopped. *Memento mori.*

She put the watch back in her pocket, and put her hand over her heart: it had been a strange dream tonight, thinking of what never could have been—her final adventures in Wonderland.

She had never quite nerved herself up to do it, in the end. Only dreamed.

And now? Now was she brave enough?

The painting was still there, her ending was near—she could feel it.

Tonight, would she give in to the temptation to climb up onto a chair, and then painfully onto the fireplace, risking a fall—only to find that she could not go through, that it had always been an illusion?

A dream?

She had waited too long; her terrible, imperious curiosity had finally burnt out.

She began to walk toward the doorway, to go into the moon-bathed hallway to look in the mirror, and then to climb laboriously upstairs to her room, to lie back in bed, and to wait for an ending. One day it would come. Not today, she thought. A little while longer.

Then she heard the sound, quite soft, like a heartbeat.

She almost reached into her pocket, but stopped herself.

She did not want to be sure.

Just one more moment of not knowing—one more moment of the sound of an old ghost.

Really, she was becoming *too* sentimental in her old age. Almost mystical.

She turned back to the picture. The solid fastness of Tom Quad's green grass and flowing fountain beckoned to her—she thought she saw movement in the corner of the painting. A rabbit.

The watch continued to tick.

She smiled.

In the morning—just after dawn—the servants found her and carried her up to bed before calling the doctor. She had only just passed; her body was still warm, and it had not yet stiffened.

A chair stood in front of the fireplace; it almost seemed as if she had climbed up on it and tumbled, but there were no cuts or bruises upon her body, and no one had heard the sound of her falling. The servants had risen by then;

the cook had been in the kitchen, preparing breakfast for the house at the time. No one had seen her up and about; she was found by the butler, who had seen the chair out of place and come in to replace it.

The servants who washed her up and prepared her for burial after the doctor had come and gone and written out his certificate (no mention was made of the odd location in which they had found her) said for years that they had received a terrible turn: when they took the old pocket-watch out of her hand, the late Mrs. Hargreaves seemed to clutch at it, and they thought for a moment that they heard her heart beating, terribly loud, echoing all throughout the house. Even the butler heard it.

But it was only rigor mortis settling in, and only the ticking of Mrs. Hargreaves' old watch, which was given to Carryl—a watch which, unless it has stopped, still works to this day.